THE MYSTERIOUS

CORRESPONDENT

MARCEL PROUST

THE MYSTERIOUS CORRESPONDENT

· *New Stories* ·

Translated by Charlotte Mandell

A Oneworld Book

First published by Oneworld Publications in 2021
Reprinted, 2021

Originally published in French by Éditions de Fallois as *Le Mystérieux Correspondant et autres nouvelles inédites*, 2019

Copyright © Éditions de Fallois 2019
English translation copyright © Charlotte Mandell 2021
Introduction copyright © Luc Fraisse 2019

ISBN 978-1-78607-924-4
eISBN 978-0-86154-015-0

Typeset by Tetragon, London
Printed and bound in Great Britain by Clays Ltd, Elcograf
S.p.A.

Oneworld Publications
10 Bloomsbury Street
London WC1B 3SR
England

Stay up to date with the latest books,
special offers, and exclusive content from
Oneworld with our newsletter

Sign up on our website
oneworld-publications.com

Contents

Introduction

by Luc Fraisse
Professor at the University of Strasbourg

It is not very often that one unearths stories written by Marcel Proust, stories that no one had ever heard of before.

In 1978, Gallimard published the booklet *L'Indifférent*. It was discovered by Philip Kolb, editor of Proust's correspondence, thanks to letters from a late-nineteenth-century newspaper. For a long time, the text was forgotten – at least by readers – since the writer remembered it perfectly when, much later, he composed the 'Swann in Love' section in *Swann's Way*, the first volume of *In Search of Lost Time*.

The case is even more striking today, since it is a question of a whole series of stories, composed at the same time as *L'Indifférent*, the time of *Pleasures and Days*, but that have not been published:[1] Proust kept drafts of the manuscripts in his archives and didn't mention them to anyone, at least according to the various documents known to us today.

What do these stories contain? Why did Proust not speak of them to anyone? And given his apparent interest in keeping them to himself, why were they even written?

While all those enigmas cannot be resolved once and for all, one can learn something about them through their subject matter, since almost all these texts deal with the question of homosexuality. Some, like texts already known, transpose the question Proust is concerned with into female homosexuality. Others have no transposition. No doubt their young author chose to keep these revealing stories, which were probably too scandalous at the time, secret. But he did feel the need to write them. They comprise, hiding in plain sight, the *private diary* the writer entrusted to no one.

What could have caused a scandal in Proust's time, in relation to his family milieu, in relation to his society, is the very fact of homosexuality. For these stories contain nothing obscene, nothing that would give rise to voyeurism. They explore, by extraordinarily varied paths as we will see, the *psychological and moral* subject of homosexuality. They

---

[1] Except for 'A Captain's Reminiscence': see below, the introduction to that story, the manuscript of which is examined and presented here for the first time.

essentially reveal a psychology of suffering. They do not invite us to intrude on Proust's private life; rather, they lead us to understand a human experience.

Coming from the archives compiled by Bernard de Fallois, who died in January 2018, these stories require a little history to shed light on why they have waited so long for publication, and in what context Proust wrote or drafted them, then once and for all removed them from the public gaze, and even from his own close confidants.

There was a time – now long forgotten – when if one looked at Marcel Proust's literary fate, one could be forgiven for thinking that this writer had lived a life that was essentially split in half: a youth spent in the *salons*, flower in his buttonhole; and an adulthood devoted to the single-minded writing of a vast work whose completion he barely had time to glimpse in the distance when he died at the age of fifty-one.

Marcel Proust, the author of *In Search of Lost Time*, that great monument of French literature, that work of world-wide heritage. His contemporaries realized his importance as the successive volumes appeared, culminating in the last books in 1927. But evaluating the magnitude of the cycle of novels was left till later, since it was too immense and too rich to be assimilated right away. Whatever the case, its author had died while still working on it, at the same age as Balzac and for much the same reasons. Wasn't it inconsiderate (the thinking went) that Proust chose to wait for the beginning of his physical decline before he settled down to this superhuman literary undertaking, writing almost nothing, like the hero of *In Search of Lost Time* up to *Time Regained*?

Without *In Search of Lost Time*, what would Marcel Proust amount to? A minor work from his youth, *Pleasures and Days*, published at the end of the nineteenth century – leaving it to us to turn the page of the twentieth century to see the literary genius of his *magnum opus* suddenly appear. A few translations of Ruskin, not unconnected to the master work that would follow, since they centred on cathedrals and on reading. But nothing more. One uneven book, one writer as translator.

This school of thought began to shift in the middle of the century. In 1949 André Maurois published, with Hachette, a book called *In Search of Marcel Proust*, which lets us breathe the atmosphere in which the novelist evolved through his great work. From correspondence, the biographer drew statements suggesting that this 'last-minute miracle writer of Literature' had been all the while, constantly, concerned with writing. Maurois met a young graduate student, Bernard de Fallois, who wanted to write, if the Faculté de Paris accepted him, a thesis devoted to Proust, and in the wake of his own research Maurois introduced

Fallois to the writer's niece, Suzy Mante-Proust, devoted, like her late father, to Proust's heritage.

Even before opening the family archives, and later on searching through the wealth of sales catalogues, Bernard de Fallois was sceptical when faced with the widely accepted idea that Proust had somehow composed a monument of literature all of a sudden, after emerging from a uniquely idle youth. Already, the works that preceded *In Search of Lost Time*, far from insignificant, were enough to suggest a constant progression in Proust of pre-Proust, particularly when one considered his other creative influences. This leads us to suppose that the *salon habitué* was nothing like Charles Swann, but devoted himself, rather, to intense questionings about what he could write.

In this light, the writings that came before *In Search*, from *Pleasures and Days* (1896) to Proust's translations of Ruskin's *The Bible of Amiens* (1904) and *Sesame and Lilies* (1906), should not be viewed as the dregs of the great work, but rather as harbouring an abundance of literary experimentations. These books are laboratories; the texts palpitate like matter in fusion. Their dates, however, are very far apart, leading us to imagine that the developing writer interrupted his researches and interrogations, continually putting them off till another year and resuming if and when the opportunity presented itself. Between these well-known works that we already knew about, there is a void. A void that is certainly due not to the creator's inactivity, but to our own ignorance.

The Proust family archives were only deposited at the Bibliothèque Nationale in 1962. In the hands of Bernard de Fallois – a methodical researcher with an archivist's perseverance – previously unknown papers, which soon added up to a considerable collection, came to light. Fallois pieced together a large novel in separate parts, paradoxically written in the third person though it was so close to the author's biography, the sections of which could be classified by following the chronology of the life of the character who would give the collection its title, *Jean Santeuil*. This large reconstructed novel, published by Gallimard in 1952, contained a preface by André Maurois. The letters and papers around it show that it was composed mainly between 1895 and 1899. Far from falling back into inertia, Proust had settled down to a large novel at a time when *Pleasures and Days* hadn't even been published yet. This long and ultimately unfinished new novel was, in fact, composed immediately after the completion of *Pleasures and Days*, and was apparently written without respite, as evidenced by the dates noted on the chronologically labelled texts.

Jean Santeuil, then, was the bridge between *Pleasures and Days* and John Ruskin. But now other manuscripts, other notebooks were beginning to appear. They could be placed at the threshold of *In Search*, around 1908, and they revealed that this novelistic cycle was born at the same time as an essay by Proust, polemical but philosophically well argued, against Sainte-Beuve's biographical methods. Proust sometimes thought about detaching this essay from his rough drafts and publishing it separately. But the reality of these drafts was quite different: it was an essay and a novel *at the same time*.

This hybrid composition challenged the usual critical classifications – but it didn't bother Bernard de Fallois in the least. He had already reinterpreted *Pleasures and Days* (the book Proust didn't like because it wasn't *In Search*, and because all pieces within it are disparate) as an ensemble that was, on the contrary, coherent, rich and varied. All the pieces in it hold together, each one is necessary and prepares the way for the next thing. Thus the one who discovered new books by Proust was not bothered by this essay of literary theory turning into a novel, where a well-ordered refutation of Sainte-Beuve is mingled with the Guermantes' thoughts on the novels of Balzac.

Fallois published this collection, not rearranged by prejudices of reading, in 1954, under the title (suggested by Proust in his letters of the time) *Against Sainte-Beuve*. What a paradox, Fallois would later point out, to reveal this little book of Proust's against the biographical critic, at a time when contemporary scholars were just beginning to become interested in Proust precisely from a biographical perspective. On the other hand, the time was well chosen, since during the same years, the reign of literary history, which approached criticism by restoring writers to their contemporary circumstances (what they read, their milieu, the literary schools of the time, and all the circumstances of their lives), was beginning its decline, challenged by a school that demanded a reading of the works by themselves for their internal structure. What a blessing to receive Marcel Proust's caution against biography! While he himself didn't subscribe wholly to this theory, Bernard de Fallois would retain the main lesson of the essay he revealed to the public. In his *Seven Lectures on Marcel Proust*, he asks: 'Is Proust's life as interesting as all that?' – and his reply was a definite 'No'.

The pioneer of Proust studies pursued his task, which would become his thesis. If the university allowed it, the subject of his thesis would be 'Proust's Creative Evolution up to *In Search of Lost Time*'. This thesis never saw the light of day, and was abandoned after the two major publications of Proust's works that opened up the publishing world to their discoverer. Two sections were eventually completely rewritten, and were read by Bernard de Fallois' intellectual peers. While the first part is apparently lost, the second part (which, alas, has become secondary) constitutes an entirely autonomous essay that Les Belles-Lettres published under the title *Proust avant Proust*. A scholarly essay, but one in which science is subsumed by intellectual attentiveness as a thesis ideally should be, as those theses are that go on to become perennially fashionable books. An essay whose striking originality and novelty have not been dulled by having been neglected for two generations before being brought to our knowledge today.

Fallois' exploration of *Pleasures and Days* was nourished by these ample archives, whose nuances the classifier handled like organ stops. Like Proust the detractor of Sainte-Beuve, and even, paradoxically, like Sainte-Beuve in fact, Fallois knew that the author's biography should not be absent from our reading of his works – but it should be an inner biography, which the best contemporaries of Proust called a *psychological biography*. One must know how to glimpse, in the seeming randomness of circumstances that have been lived through, the enriching perspective of structures as they emerge.

It is this structural gaze that Bernard de Fallois brings to bear on the seemingly disparate pieces gathered together in *Pleasures and Days*. What becomes clear from this retrospective study is one single search, one literary attempt – what might be called a young writer's *search for his voice* – a search that is so difficult to carry out that one must take many different paths to be able to reach one single goal. Fallois pushed clairvoyance to the point of not only identifying what, in Proust's youthful writings, prepared the still-remote *In Search of Lost Time*, but also noting a number of stances that we would never see again in Proust's later writings, because this *never again*, this *one time only*, teaches us much about the development of a Proust who has reached his full maturity.

As the essayist was pondering the long-term development of the writer's style and thought processes while he was indexing and classifying the archives, he encountered, fluttering around *Pleasures and Days*, handwritten pages that were not part of the 1896 collection, and were not published in journals of the time. Some of them appeared named in handwritten tables of contents he came across, with an eye to this very book, which Proust first called *Le Château de Réveillon* (in reference to Mme Lemaire's manor house in the Marne, where some of these texts were composed in close collaboration with Reynaldo Hahn). These were pieces that Proust moved around, added to or removed in much the same way Guillaume Apollinaire did when he put together his poetry collection *Alcools* in 1912.

These prose texts on separate pieces of paper were all short stories. Written at the same time as the ones in *Pleasures and Days* with which we are familiar, they inevitably share some similarities. But taken individually, since the author withheld them from publication, they also have a further significance as a series of unpublished pieces.

Part of Bernard de Fallois' essay speaks about this specific question. Jean-Claude Casanova wisely pre-published this part in No. 163 of the literary journal *Commentaire*, in the autumn of 2018, under the title 'Le secret et l'aveu' [The secret and the confession]. For that is the crux of the thing. But what crux, precisely?

The writings that Proust left in the margins or set aside while he was preparing his collection *Pleasures and Days* imply that it could have been a much larger book. But if its young author had included all the texts that we are reproducing here, in their finished form, the portrayal of homosexuality would have become the main subject of the book. Proust did not want this, no doubt fearing questions this might raise over his own sexuality (questions that a modern-day reader has long been able to answer). Perhaps some of these texts were of greater personal significance than of public value. Perhaps too the writer wanted to preserve a more deliberate diversity within his collection. Finally, he may have doubted the quality and the literary success of these texts that he ended up setting aside.

Proust, as a young man and a young writer, viewed homosexuality as a curse and cause of much suffering. This cannot be dismissed as merely symptomatic of mainstream opinion at the time. After all, Proust's position was entirely opposed to that of his contemporary André

Gide, hedonist and egotist, who did not embrace such an avowal of Proustian tragedy, but on the contrary associated homosexuality with vitalist happiness. Whence also arose another contrast, between a Proust torn between secrecy and disclosure, working out an elaborate system of transpositions, and a Gide who insisted on saying *I*, to such an extent that he noted in his *Journal*, after a visit to Proust in 1921: 'When I say a word or two about my Memoirs: "You can tell anything," [Proust] exclaims; "but on condition that you never say: *I*." But that won't suit me.'[2]

Proust, then, would never say *I* in such a context; but the story of the captain ('A Captain's Reminiscence') narrated in the first person is the one that comes closest to a direct, personal utterance. In these discarded stories, we see as never before a whole series of *projections* being elaborated, of discourse by proxy. The drama would be played out between two women – and although the narrator appears to be on the side of the 'innocent' woman, the story draws no facile distinction between guilt and innocence. The crucial drama of adolescence is transposed into a premature *end of life* – an *apocalypse*, in the double sense of a revelation of the end of days for the character, and also of the act of revealing implied in the Greek word *apocaluptein*.

---

2   André Gide, entry for 14 May 1921, in *Journals, Vol. 2: 1914–1927*, translated by Justin O'Brien, New York, Alfred A. Knopf, 1948, p. 265.

The suffering of being condemned to not being loved by the person one loves is transposed into a musical universe ('After Beethoven's Eighth Symphony'). Suffering is also transposed into the situation of a heroine who knows she is condemned to her disease but who decides to live out her agony with insouciance ('Pauline de S.'). Suffering is externalized as a cat-squirrel that accompanies the man, at his home and outside in society, unbeknownst to anyone ('The Awareness of Loving Her'). Finally, suffering can even be reassigned as a 'Gift of the Fairies'...

But transposition, when it bears such a heavy personal and emotional weight, is not easy. The narrator to whom Proust delegates the action of the story gets mixed up in it. We will see how the roles of Françoise and Christiane are confused and interchanged in the manuscript of 'The Mysterious Correspondent'. The gift of the fairies (which is to accept suffering in exchange for the gift of experiencing real emotions) is accepted with more resignation than conviction. The secret animal, destined to accompany the unrequited lover of 'The Awareness of Loving Her' throughout his life, brings the subject a consolation that does not erase the failure. The contradiction is not resolved.

Christian morality, Catholic in this instance, weighs heavily on these explorations in a way that is absent from Proust's later work. What we read in *Pleasures and Days*, as the collection was published, reduces religious concern to a superficial whiff of mysticism surrounded by a halo of decadent, *fin-de-siècle* melancholy. These discarded stories, on the other hand, are more insistent. Christiane is going to die from consumption for having silently burned with love for her friend Françoise. Françoise asks if giving in to Christiane's desire would save her. Her confessor replies that it would mean causing the dying woman (who has been presented to the priest as a dying man) to lose by one deed the sacrifice of an entire life in order to fulfil some ideal of purity. The two positions are radically opposed: in terms of absolute value, neither of the two possibilities is invalidated.

The young author of these stories will never again utter with the same insistence this *memento mori* of classical sermons. He will no longer take God to task as Creator (except through images portraying artistic creation) to ask him *why*. Here the suffering character, isolated from the world of love, utters a very personal *'my kingdom is not of this world'*; he wonders where he can find for himself that promise of *'peace on Earth to men of good will'*. The dialogue of the dead in 'In the Underworld' distances the distressing closeness of all these questions, but the ancient patina of the Underworld does not erase the perspective of Hell or Christian damnation, which one of the protagonists tries to ward off by calling poetry (and thus poets) *felix culpa* ('oh happy fault', the phrase used in a hymn to describe original sin).

The doctor characters, halfway between Adrien Proust, the writer's father, and the future Docteur du Boulbon, fictional doctor of *In Search*, take over to open a possible way towards what Bergson, after Proust's death, would call 'the two sources of morality and religion'. Christiane's doctor, by emphasizing that his patient is dying from a kind of consumption that does not stem from any organic cause, anticipates Freud visiting Jean-Martin Charcot at La Salpêtrière and preparing his *Studies on Hysteria*. 'A Captain's Reminiscence' suggests the case of a character who is unaware of his own homosexuality, even as he describes it in a story where it will never be named outright. 'After Beethoven's Eighth Symphony' meditates on the relationship between an asthmatic's breathing and the occupation of space.

But homosexual psychology, or homosexuality seen from within, whether directly or transposed, does not even remotely constitute the sole concern of these stories. In these stories we can see the writer at a time when his literary undertaking, which would continue to take shape up to *In Search*, was beginning.

The student of philosophy is not far off; he is in fact quite contemporary with the writer. The consolation for not being loved, projected into a musical universe ('After Beethoven's Eighth Symphony'), seems already nourished by the metaphysics of Schopenhauer's music. The captain, in his laborious reminiscence, repeats the very Fichte-ean distinction of the self and non-self, and his still-clumsy questioning about the re-creation of the past in his thinking is not without great promise, very like the search for a definition of *essence*. These reminders of Proust's philosophical erudition are already discreet; the mature Proust of *In Search* will find a way to enrich his prose with them without making them over-evident.

As we might expect, some of the annotations here give us a fleeting insight into what would eventually form the basis of major episodes in the still-remote *In Search of Lost Time*. Here we will see the role of literature appear in the resurrection of characters: the mediation of Botticelli in the apprehension of the beloved; the two lines by Alfred de Vigny that will serve as epigraph to *Sodom and Gomorrah* ('In the Underworld'); perhaps the anticipated explanation of Saint-Loup's cold salute at the end of the Doncières episode in *The Guermantes Way*; a first version of the great controversy about homosexuality between Charlus and Brichot (here Caylus and Renan in dialogue in 'In the Underworld') in *The Captive*; but also what the Docteur du Boulbon's tirade in *The Guermantes Way* on the pathologies of creative geniuses will one day answer; a first version of the solitary promenade in the Bois du Boulogne that will one day serve as the closing scene in *Swann's Way* ('Jacques Lefelde'); as well as an early version of the episode of the 'new writer' in *The Guermantes Way*; and the etymology of the rhetorical exclamation 'Trees, you have nothing more to say to me' at the heart of *Time Regained*.

The reader can make out traces of the budding writer's own literary preferences here: Racine's *Phaedra* and Victor Hugo's 'Olympio's Sadness'; perhaps Stendhal in 'Jacques Lefelde' and Dumas *père* in 'In the Underworld'; much of the world of Edgar Allan Poe between the lines as we'll see, and in this realm the reminiscences of Gérard de Nerval and the novels of Tolstoy, whose influence would become more remote after *Jean Santeuil*.

For the writing of these stories allows us a glimpse of the young writer experimenting with literary forms that he will set aside before maturing in his craft: the unresolved story, the fantastic tale, the dialogue of the dead. More precisely, it is interesting to note how borrowing freely from the forms of parable, apologue and fairytale here allows the novelist-in-training to pick and choose those forms he will retain, and those he will set aside as he develops his own style.

Proust borrowed especially from the society novel, whose underlying current is not emphasized enough in the atmosphere of *In Search of Lost Time*, and which is made up of swift microcosms in several of his stories, especially the lovers' meeting in the context of high society, with its resources but especially its obstacles. This society novel, with its concentrated atmosphere, makes economical use of his long study of the novelistic arsenal even within a lengthy novel, but more appropriately at the service of the brevity of a short story. This world of salons, maître d's, excursions, fiacres: this will be Swann's world. Proust will discover this universe in the novel of his friend Georges de Lauris, *Ginette Chatenay*, which Proust read in manuscript form from 1908 to 1909, and which was subsequently published in 1910, and portrays a heroine who is reading *Pleasures and Days*. The circle is closed.

So many stages of learning and experimentation separate the young writer of these stories from the novelist of *In Search* that we might expect to find nothing of the latter in this novitiate. From that point of view, it is interesting to isolate precisely what we can already detect in these stories. For instance, here we find the very first versions of the future rift between time lost and time regained, which here are called frivolity and profundity, scatteredness and inwardness, appearance and reality. This rift would soon be explored more deeply in *Jean Santeuil* – but even then, it will not be thought of as a structuring divide, and this large novel that followed the short stories will fail because it was unable to expound on this idea in a structurally meaningful way.

These stories also witness the birth of the narrator of *In Search* in his capacity to see through appearances – to recognize (as the ever-present La Bruyère in *Pleasures and Days* would say) the man we do not see through the man we see – to which we can attribute the cheerfulness of a dying woman; the inexplicable tuberculosis of another; the sad, anguished memory of a captain; the solitary, repetitive strolls of a writer at the same time every day in the Bois.

In the perpetually changing universe of a writer, phrases also have their history, or rather, their own genesis and development. Some far-off day, the *stamp of authenticity* will condense a famous passage from *Time Regained*. It was in an unpublished story from his youth that Proust saw this resource born from his pen.

We may think that some of these stories were not successful because their author hesitated, and couldn't decide among several possibilities. Take the captain, for instance. At first he appears to remember the past perfectly well; but in the very next sentence he can't manage to recall the corporal who had so moved him many years ago. Elsewhere, we'll see direct dialogue and narrative analysis clash over the subject of the story, without either of the two forms managing to take precedence.

These hesitations were, in fact, fertile. For these contradictions were all temporary. We, who can today read not only *In Search of Lost Time* but also the notebooks in which it was drafted, we know that the novelist would proceed in this way, juxtaposing on the same page a situation in the story and its opposite, because he wanted to experiment with the impact of each, its implications, and the analysis it could give rise to. The notebooks of *The Fugitive* are significant for this issue: it is here that we read that Albertine knew – but did not really know – Mlle Vinteuil and her friend; that she had – but perhaps actually she hadn't – had relations with Andrée; the hero does not at all want to know with whom Gilberte used to walk up the Champs-Élysées – and yet he asks her. The writer of *In Search*, who would weigh all the potentialities of his narrative, is already hidden inside the contradictions of these unpublished stories.

A moral problem is revealed here in a sombre atmosphere. Not just that: these stories tell of wonder confronted with beauty, the denseness of life enclosed in mystery, enigmas to be solved, and the inalienable wealth each person possesses, which is the exploration of his or her inner world; art prepares us, accompanies us, completes this undertaking for us. In this way, from his earliest writings, Proust offers this reversal that Albert Camus (the Camus of *The Rebel*) would read in *Time Regained* – an alternative to despair.

Even the curse and the suffering are revealed to be creative: they are the things that put the situations and characters in place, that deepen the questionings, that necessitate the original, ever-renewed and modulated transpositions. This young writer, who both reveals and conceals his secret, seems already to foreshadow the Gilberte or Albertine of his future work. For if they were to repay all the love borne for them a hundredfold, hiding nothing and revealing everything, they would annihilate the analytic force by which the narrator of *In Search* triumphs. Because, as he would go on to reveal in *Time Regained*, 'ideas are substitutes for sorrows'.

L.F.

Acknowledgements

This volume of unpublished stories would not have been possible without the confidence entrusted to this undertaking by Dominique Goust, head of the Éditions de Fallois. All my thanks and gratitude go to him and his editorial team.

L.F.

Note on the Text

We are reproducing here a series of handwritten and, with one exception, unpublished texts by Marcel Proust, all from the archives of Bernard de Fallois (dossiers 1.1 and 5.1 in their original index). They were used by Fallois in his study of *Pleasures and Days*, which Proust wrote at the same time as the texts included here, some of which were for a time considered part of the project. Each text is introduced with an explanation of how it came to be written, and with a few remarks on the novelties it presents and its longer-term influence in Proust's later work. We are presenting these texts in simplified transcription, but accompanied by an exhaustive summary of variations in the footnotes; the italicized words in the footnotes are alternative phrases that Proust added in the margins of the manuscripts. In our introductions, we refer to the following editions of Proust:

– *À la recherche du temps perdu*, edited by Jean-Yves Tadié, Paris, Gallimard, 'Bibliothèque de la Pléiade', 4 vols, 1987–9.

– *Correspondance de Marcel Proust*, edited, annotated and introduced by Philip Kolb, Paris, Plon, 21 vols, 1970–93.

– *Les Plaisirs et les Jours, Jean Santeuil*, edited by Pierre Clarac and Yves Sandre, Paris, Gallimard, 'Bibliothèque de la Pléiade', 1971.

[Original edition of *Jean Santeuil* by Bernard de Fallois, preface by André Maurois, Paris, Gallimard, 3 vols, 1952.]

– *Contre Sainte-Beuve, Pastiches et Mélanges, Essais et articles*, edited by Pierre Clarac and Yves Sandre, Paris, Gallimard, 'Bibliothèque de la Pléiade', 1971.

[Original edition of *Contre Sainte-Beuve suivi de Nouveaux Mélanges*, according to a different arrangement, preface by Bernard de Fallois, Paris, Gallimard, 1954.]

– *Carnets*, edited by Florence Callu and Antoine Compagnon, Paris, Gallimard, 2002.

L.F.

PAULINE DE S.

[This brief moral tale belongs to the end-of-life stories that appear prominently in Pleasures and Days, *as well as in the discarded texts following it that you will read here. More light-hearted than those texts, this one leans towards a favourite message of sermons (especially classical ones), the* memento mori. *As in the two unpublished stories that follow this one, it's the character of the doctor who seems to raise the religious questions. Near the beginning we find outlined, in a still early but decisive rough draft, the rift between time lost and time regained. As part of the classic opposition between the humorous and the serious, frivolity and moral gravitas, the rift is directed towards 'the depths of emotion in the arts, where we feel ourselves descending into the very heart of our being', which foretells the aesthetic morality of the Proust of* In Search, *a concept particularly reflected in the posthumous septet Vinteuil mysteriously delivers to the hero in* The Captive *(À la recherche du temps perdu, Vol. III, p. 753 ff.). The serious readings that Pauline rejects, in particular* The Imitation of Christ, *provide the sources for the epigraphs to the*

pieces in this collection; instead of Labiche, whom the heroine favours here, the author prefers 'Fragments of Italian Comedy'. Might the young author of Pleasures and Days *be one of those who has seen death up close, yet who has nonetheless returned, under his* fin-de-siècle *veneer, to his frivolous activities and thoughts? Thus the situation of this seemingly straightforward piece is not entirely decipherable at first glance.]*

I learned one day that my old friend Pauline de S.,[1] who had long ago been diagnosed with cancer, would not last the year, and that she realized this so clearly that the doctor, incapable of[2] deceiving her strong intelligence, had confessed the truth to her.[3] But she also knew that, up until the last month[4] and unless some unforeseen accident should befall her (an ever-present possibility), she would keep her presence of mind and even a certain physical activity.[5] Now that I knew her last illusions had vanished, it was extremely difficult for me to go and see her. I decided, however,[6] one evening to go there the next day. That evening[7] I could not fall asleep. Things seemed to me now

---

1   Draft: S. *who had slowly succumbed to cancer.*

2   Draft: incapable of *outsmarting.*

3   Var.: the doctor *had ceased outsmarting her.*

4   Var.: *day.*

5   Draft: physical activity. *I took a long time [before I] decided to go and see her.*

6   Draft: however. *Since the day before things appear[ed] to me.*

7   *That evening*: interlinear addition.

the way they must have seemed to her, so close to death, the opposite of how they usually appear to us. Pleasures, entertainments, lives,[8] special, even insignificant, labours – all seemed insipid, laughable, ridiculously, terrifyingly small and unreal. Meditations on life and on the soul, the depths of emotion in the arts, where we feel ourselves descending into the very heart of our being, goodness, forgiveness, pity, charity, repentance foregrounded, seemed the only real things. Enlarged, I arrived at her home,[9] in one of those minutes when one feels inside oneself nothing but the soul,[10] the soul that was overflowing, unconcerned with anything else, ready to weep. I went in. She was seated at her usual armchair near the window[11] and her face was not imprinted with the sadness it had worn for some days in my imagination.[12] Her thinness, her sickly pallor were purely physical. Her features had kept their mocking expression.[13] She[14] was holding in her hand[15] a

---

8   *lives*: interlinear addition.

9   Var.: *my soul enlarged*.

10   Var.: *feeling inside myself* nothing but the soul.

11   Var.: near *the fire*.

12   Var.: *solemn sadness with which my imagination endowed her*.

13   Draft: mocking expression. *Once my initial surprise had passed, it was quite easily explained*.

14   Draft: She *was in the process of holding*.

15   Var.: *à la main* [not *en main*].

political pamphlet[16] that she set down when I came in. We chatted for an hour. The scintillating conversation went on as it had in the past, at the expense of various people she knew.[17] She was only stopped by a coughing fit after which she spat a little blood. When she had recovered she said: 'Leave,[18] dear friend, I'm anxious not to be tired tonight, since I'm having some friends over for dinner. But let's try to see each other these coming days. Get a box for a matinee. The theatre at night is too tiring for me.' 'For which play?' I asked. 'Any one you like, so long as it isn't your boring *Hamlet* or *Antigone*,[19] you know my tastes, a cheerful play, by Labiche if they're doing one now, or if not, an operetta.' I left, astonished. More visits taught me that reading[20] the Gospels, or *The Imitation of Christ*, music and poetry, meditations, repentance[21] for insults made or[22] forgiveness for insults received, conversations with scholars, priests, dear friends or former enemies, or conversations with herself, were all absent from this home where she was ending her life. I am not speaking of the bodily self-pity

---

16 Var.: *a book by Labiche*; draft: *and one day next to her* a political pamphlet *was still open*.

17 Draft: she knew. *She only stopped*.

18 Draft: *go away*.

19 *so long as it isn't…*: interlinear addition.

20 *reading*: interlinear addition.

21 Var.: *forgiveness*.

22 Draft: or *repentances*.

that she was too hearty and too tough to feel.[23] Often I wondered if it was a pose,[24] a mask, if a part[25] of her life that she hid from me[26] was in fact her true nature. I have learned since that this was not the case, that with others and even alone[27] she was with me as *before*. It seemed to me that there was a hardening here, a singular aberration. O how foolish I was, I who saw death so close up and yet who resumed my frivolous life. What was it that surprised me, that I didn't already have in front of my eyes?[28] All of us as we are,[29] hasn't the doctor condemned us all,[30] are we not unaware of that, that we[31] will certainly die? Yet we see many who[32] meditate on death in order to leave life with dignity.

---

23 Draft: *I could not understand it and.*

24 Var.: *comedy.*

25 Var.: *an unknown* part.

26 Var.: *us.*

27 Var.: *all* alone.

28 Var.: that I did not *constantly see.*

29 Draft: are, *that we are nothing but.*

30 Draft: all *and what else could we do.*

31 Draft: *we are going to.*

32 Draft: who *prepare themselves.*

THE MYSTERIOUS

CORRESPONDENT

[This complete story, which was for a time included in Pleasures and Days *and was then dedicated to the pianist Léon Delafosse (1874–1955), despite a few unfinished details, has this in common with other published stories: avowing the unavowable at the approach of death, an approach that reshuffles all the cards and unburdens the secret of all its moral weight.*

The title is reiterated once during the story, and indicates that everything occurs via letters mysteriously found in the apartment of the heroine, Françoise, who imagines these letters come from a soldier.

Around this same time, during the summer of 1893, Proust and some friends began to write an epistolary novel, in which Proust took on the role of a society lady in love with a non-commissioned officer: she opens up to her confessor (whose role was played by Daniel Halévy, with Louis de La Salle taking that of an officer; see Correspondance, *Vol. IV, pp. 413–21). This novel, written by many hands, was never finished, but while he was writing his part, Proust composed another story, possibly in secret, in which Françoise's confessor, the Abbé de Tresves, appears only in the final pages. The main part of this story is a non-epistolary narrative.*

The mysteriously appearing letters indirectly evoke Edgar Allan Poe's story 'The Purloined Letter', which Proust admired (see Correspondance, *Vol. X, p. 292). Something from Poe's* Extraordinary Tales *also occurs in Proust's story, through the dying woman (Christiane) who at one point transmits her consumption to her friend Françoise. The same half-light that occurs at the heart of the story echoes Nerval's opposition between reality and dream (in one variation, it's a question of a* second life).

This story from Proust's youth lets us glimpse the budding novelist trying out formulas for a story that he would only rarely use later on. Near the beginning, he tries to convey all his character's psychology through the carefully wrought description of her hands (we are reminded of Charles Bovary's famous hat). Soon after, Proust (clumsily) attempts suspense writing, about the letters found in Françoise's dining room. Here we can see sentences crossed out and interlinear additions that reveal in the narrator a certain difficulty in setting up and describing the necessary narrative situations. This difficulty would remain in the author of In Search, *where many a sentence is weighed down because it is a matter of justifying, in a concrete situation that is difficult to set in place, the reflection at which the narrator seeks to arrive.*

In In Search, *a letter will appear from a mysterious correspondent: the telegram that the hero of* The Fugitive *receives as he is about to leave for Venice, signed 'Albertine', who is, in fact, dead (Vol. IV, pp. 220–23) – there had been a confusion with the name 'Gilberte', who is announcing her wedding. The whole of this old short story seems to be condensed into that telegram. In the same volume, another mysterious correspondent will intervene, from whom the hero receives a letter after his article has been published in* Le Figaro: *'I received another letter besides the one from Mme Goupil, but the name, Sautton, was unknown to me. The writing was uneducated, the language charming. I was vexed I couldn't find out who had written to me' (Vol. IV, p. 170). We know that this circumstance, purposely made obscure, was inspired by a letter sent to Proust by Alfred Agostinelli in 1907, after the publication of Proust's article 'Impressions de route en automobile' (see* Correspondance, *Vol. VII, p. 315). But the schema of this mysterious circumstance is much older, as we see here, in Proust the novelist's imagination.*

We also see here for the first time from Proust's pen the stamp *of* authenticity *that we will see reappear at the other end of the novelist's writings, at the end of* Time Regained. *There, the dogmatic narrator of the section called 'Perpetual Adoration' declares, on the subject of involuntary memories: 'their main characteristic was that I was not free to choose them; they were given to me as is. And I felt that must be the stamp of their authenticity' (Vol. IV, p. 457). Proof that an expression is never lost but can survive for an exceptionally long time, if it forever fixes in place the concept the writer is patiently forging.*

A story in the form of an enigma, the fable takes place in the atmosphere of a society novel to portray homosexuality, here through Gomorrah. The issues at play will be love not shared, the weighty feeling of guilt, the relationship between secrecy and avowal, the burden of social judgement and the relationship between morality and (Catholic) religion.

Since the female correspondent has to disguise herself as a male correspondent, while Proust transposes what he knows of homosexuality into the secret tragedy of a woman, complex ambiguities result. What's more, we will observe the constant confusion of first names from the author's pen: Françoise and Christiane are constantly interchanged, which causes frequent crossings-out and even some omissions. The secret of the enigma is involuntarily given away – a slip of Proust's pen – by a feminine form of the past participle (vue) to designate the mysterious correspondent quite early on. Even the secret and the avowal are found to be reversed: it is the woman who holds an unavowable secret who confesses it in her letters; and the woman who receives the letter, and who has nothing to hide, is in the grip of the secret.

A certain parody of classical orators and preachers runs through Proust's evocations of Catholic piety. The priest intervenes, as in Les Liaisons dangereuses, *at the crisis of the drama. The whiff of the edifying novel evaporates under the effect of a twofold questioning of moral precepts, seeming to be on a different wavelength from the drama, and maintaining the weight of a deadly guilt. Still, the sublime sacrifice the confessor advocates, which Christiane will in fact carry out, remains profound.*

Faced with the demands of God, the doctor's precepts serve here as an excuse to force open and penetrate the secret. The thesis defended is that a certain amount of suffering, with its consequences, requires one to go beyond the rules of morality. Note that the doctor's reminder of Christiane's state of consumption, a state that does not stem from any organic cause, strangely echoes Freud's Studies on Hysteria *(1895), carried out at La Salpêtrière with Charcot (with whom Proust's father, Adrien Proust, collaborated). According to Freud, the catatonia of hysterics does not stem from any organic deficiency, but actually results from the neutralization of a conflict between contrary, exceptionally intense forces. Although Proust, apparently, did not hear of Freud's theories until much later, he places himself intuitively at their heart from his earliest writings.]*

[Trans. note: It is interesting to note that an opera by the eighteenth-century Black composer Joseph Boulogne, Chevalier de Saint-Georges (1745–99), called L'Amant anonyme *(The Anonymous Lover), has a similar plot to this story. Valcour is secretly in love with his friend Léontine, but because of social conventions he is unable to tell her of his affections. One wonders if Proust knew of this opera, especially since the story was originally dedicated to a musician (the pianist Léon Delafosse).]*

'Dear friend, I forbid you to go home on foot, I'll have the horses harnessed, it's too cold out, you could get sick.' Françoise de Lucques[1] had said that just before as she led out her friend Christiane,[2] and now that she had gone she regretted that clumsy phrase, which would have been quite an insignificant one if it had been spoken to another[3] – it was a phrase that might have worried the invalid about her state. Seated near the fire where she was by turns[4] warming her feet and hands, she[5] kept asking herself the question that was torturing her: could Christiane[6] be cured of this wasting disease?[7]

---

1   Names crossed out: *Christiane Florence Tavens*.

2   MS: Christiane *Tavens*; *Florence de Lucques* crossed out.

3   *quite… another*: interlinear addition.

4   *by turns*: interlinear addition.

5   Draft: She *was wondering if one could cure this languidness of Françoise she felt.*

6   MS: Françoise.

7   Draft: wasting disease. *And depending on whether she [said] answered yes or no she felt all her most inviolable, her most impetuous intellectual and moral wrath, and also her gentlest and humblest. Her hands one [saw].*

They hadn't brought enough lamps. She was in the dark. But now, as she was warming her hands again, the fire illumined their grace and their soul.[8] In their resigned beauty[9] – sad exiles in this vulgar world – one could read the emotions as clearly as in a face's expression. Normally absent-minded, they lay outstretched in gentle languor. But this evening, at the risk of creasing the delicate stem[10] that bore them so nobly, they were painfully spread out[11] like tormented[12] flowers. And soon,[13] tears[14] fell from her eyes in the darkness and appeared one by one[15] the instant they touched the hands that, spread wide before the flames, were in full light. A servant entered: it was the mail, a single letter in a complicated script that Françoise[16]

---

8   Series of drafts: soul. *The sweet, delicate hands seemed borne by an and* [sic] *beautiful as flowers, nobly born on the stem of the wrist, from which they sprang in a proud line before blossoming from which they sprang as slender as she before blossoming. These hands of such great charm and of such were* [sic] *as greatly expressive as a face a gaze and suffering as a soul as expressive as a smile or a gaze. They were usually stable and beautiful suffering creatures like exiles, usually nonchalantly resting, this evening they were being painfully shaken. They were suffering in their grace.*

9   Var.: *pure* beauty.

10 Var.: *the wrist.*

11 Var.: *strangely.*

12 Var.: flowers *of despair*; draft: *and were saddened in their language.*

13 Draft: soon *caught in the little one, one saw land.*

14 Draft: tears *appeared on her.*

15 *one by one*: interlinear addition.

16 MS: Christiane.

did not recognize.[17] (Despite the fact that her husband loved Christiane as much as she did and tenderly consoled Françoise for her suffering when he noticed it, she didn't want to sadden him unnecessarily with the sight of her tears if he[18] came home unexpectedly, and she wanted to have time to wipe her eyes in[19] the darkness.) And so she ordered that lamps be brought in five minutes, and she moved the letter closer to the fire to shed light on it. The fire was burning brightly enough that Françoise[20] could make out the letters as she bent forward to illuminate it, and here is what she read.

Madame,

For a long time I have loved you but I can neither tell you nor not tell you.[21] Forgive me. Vaguely everything I have been told about your intellectual life, about the unique distinction of your soul, has convinced me[22] that in you alone I would encounter sweetness after a bitter[23] life, peace after an adventurous life, after a life of

---

17 Drafts: *She read turned around waited for them to bring went brought the letter close to the fire to be able to read and said to wait five minutes to bring the lamps.*

18 *if he came home unexpectedly*: interlinear addition.

19 Draft: *to stay* in the darkness.

20 MS: Christiane.

21 Var.: *nor go much longer without doing so.*

22 Draft: *made me imagine that you were the Chosen One who.*

23 Var.: *acrid.*

uncertainty and darkness the path towards light. And you have been my spiritual companion without knowing it.[24] *But that is no longer enough for me. It is your body I want, and unable to have it, in my despair and frenzy I write this letter to calm myself, the way one crumples a paper while waiting, the way one writes a name on the bark of a tree,*[25] *the way one cries a name into the wind or over the sea.*[26] *To lift the corner of your lips with my mouth,*[27] *I would give my life.*[28] *The thought that this might be possible*[29] *and that it is impossible both set me on fire. When you receive letters from me, you will know that I am experiencing a period when this desire is driving me mad.*[30] *You are so kind, have pity on me, I am dying for being unable to possess you.*

Françoise[31] had just finished this letter when the servant entered with the lamps, giving so to speak the sanction of reality to the letter she had read as in a dream, in the shifting, uncertain gleam of the flames. Now the soft but

24 *without knowing it*: interlinear addition.
25 Var.: on *the trees*.
26 Draft: sea. *You are*.
27 Var.: *my tongue*.
28 Var.: *all* my life.
29 Var.: this *could be* possible.
30 Var.: *this idea makes me mad and I must calm down*.
31 MS: Christiane.

certain, forthright light of the lamps[32] caused to emerge,[33] from the half-light between the facts[34] of this world and the dreams of the other, our interior world, and gave it something like the stamp of authenticity according to matter and according to life.[35] Françoise[36] wanted first to show this letter to her husband.[37] But then she thought it more generous[38] to spare him this anxiety, and that she at least owed her silence to the unknown person to whom she could give nothing else, awaiting oblivion.[39] But the next morning she received a letter[40] in the same elaborate writing with these words: 'Tonight at 9 I will be at your home.[41] I want at least to see you.' Then Françoise[42] was afraid. Christiane[43] was going to leave the next day to spend two weeks in the countryside, where the cooler air could do her good. She wrote to Christiane[44] asking

---

32 Draft: lamps *gave the most perfect placed something like the stamp of [real] life.*

33 Var.: *made that* emerge.

34 Var.: the *material* facts.

35 *and according to life*: interlinear addition.

36 MS: Christiane.

37 Draft: husband. *He was not yet.*

38 Var.: generous *for [her husband] him.*

39 Var.: *and soon if possible oblivion.*

40 Draft: letter *where it was said.*

41 Draft: home. *I love you as.*

42 Var.: *Christiane.*

43 MS: Françoise.

44 Var.: *Françoise.*

her to dine with her, since her husband was going out that evening. She ordered the servants not to let anyone else in and had all the shutters[45] solidly closed. She said nothing to Christiane,[46] but at 9 o'clock told her she had a migraine,[47] asking her to go into the *salon* near the door that led to her bedroom, and not to let anyone come in. She knelt down in her bedroom and prayed. At 9:15, feeling faint, she went into the dining room to get a little rum. On the table there was a large piece of white paper on which were printed[48] the following words: 'Why don't you want to see me? I would love you so well. Someday you will regret the hours I could have helped you pass. I beg you.[49] Allow me to see you, but[50] if you order it I will go away immediately.'[51] Françoise [was] horrified. She thought of asking her servants to come with weapons. She was ashamed of this idea, and thinking that there was no more effective authority than her own to have sway over the unknown man, she wrote on the bottom[52]

---

45 *else… shutters*: interlinear addition.

46 MS: Françoise.

47 *her… migraine*: interlinear addition. Several additions are incompatible with each other; we can make this one out: *wanted to rest a little in her room having a migraine.*

48 Var.: *with elaborate handwriting.*

49 *I beg you*: interlinear addition.

50 *but*: interlinear addition.

51 Var.: *I am going to go away.' Then Christiane was afraid.*

52 Var.: *across.*

of the paper: 'Leave immediately I order you.' And she rushed[53] into her room, threw herself onto her prie-Dieu, and prayed fervently to the Holy Virgin[54] without another thought in her mind. After[55] half an hour she went to find Christiane,[56] who was reading at her request in the living room. She wanted to have something to drink and asked her to accompany her into the dining room. She trembled as she went in, supported by Christiane, [and] almost fainted as she opened the door, then advanced with slow steps, almost dying. At each step it seemed as if she had no strength to take another, and that she would faint[57] right there and then. All of a sudden she had to stifle a cry. On the table, a new piece of paper had appeared, on which she read: 'I have obeyed. I will not come back. You will never see me again.'[58]

Fortunately Christiane,[59] alarmed by her friend's faintness,[60] hadn't seen the paper, and Françoise[61] had time to pick it up swiftly but nonchalantly and to put it in her

---

53 Var.: rushed *closing the doors*.

54 Var.: prayed to *Our Lord Jesus Christ*.

55 Var.: *Then* after.

56 MS: Françoise.

57 Var.: *stop*.

58 *I will… again*: interlinear addition.

59 Var.: *Françoise*.

60 Var.: *confusion*.

61 Var.: *Christiane*.

pocket.[62] 'You should go home early,' she said hastily to Christiane,[63] 'since you're leaving tomorrow morning.[64] Goodbye my dear friend. I might not be able to come and see you[65] tomorrow morning;[66] if you don't see me it's because I'll have slept late to cure my migraine.' (The doctor had forbidden any farewells, to prevent Christiane from becoming overly emotional.)[67] But Christiane,[68] aware of her state,[69] understood clearly[70] why Françoise didn't dare come[71] [and why] these farewells had been forbidden, and she cried while saying goodbye to Françoise, who overcame her sorrow till the end and remained calm to reassure Christiane.[72] Françoise[73] did not sleep. In the last note from the stranger the words 'You will never see me again' worried her more than anything. Since he said 'see again', she must have seen her[74] [sic]. She had the windows

---

62 Draft: pocket. *Then she said to Françoise* [sic]: *It was in order to eat a little in the hope of curing my migraine that I had you come here but it's better now, it's no matter. Let's go on. Besides.*

63 *she said hastily to Christiane*: interlinear addition.

64 Draft: morning *to spend those few days*.

65 Var.: I *will not come and see you*.

66 Draft: morning, *it will be too early for me*.

67 Var.: *Françoise*.

68 Var.: *Françoise*.

69 *aware of her state*: interlinear addition.

70 Draft: clearly *the reason*.

71 *Françoise… come*: interlinear addition.

72 Var.: *Françoise*.

73 Var.: *Christiane*.

74 Draft: her. *The next morning*.

checked: not a single shutter had moved.[75] He could not have come in that way. So he must have bribed[76] the concierge. She wanted to dismiss him then, but the following instant she felt unsure, and decided to wait.[77]

The next day, Christiane's doctor, whom Françoise had asked for news of Christiane as soon as she left, came to see her.[78] He did not hide from her that her friend's state, while not irremediably compromised, could suddenly become hopeless, and that he did not envision any precise treatment for her to follow. 'Ah, it's a great misfortune that she didn't marry,' he said.[79] 'That new life could alone have a salutary[80] influence on her languid state. Only new pleasures could modify such a profound state.' 'Get married!' Françoise cried out. 'But who would want to marry her now that she is so ill?' 'She should take a lover,' said the doctor. 'She will marry him if he cures her.' 'Don't say such awful things, Doctor,' Françoise exclaimed. 'I am not saying awful things,' the doctor replied sadly. 'When a woman is in such a state and she's a virgin, only a completely different[81] life

---

75 Var.: windows *whose shutters had been closed.*

76 Var.: *bought.*

77 Draft: She *dismissed him the next day despite.*

78 Hesitation about first names: *Christiane* written above Françoise, *Françoise* above Christiane.

79 Var.: he said, *or that she didn't take or if it's too late, that she doesn't take a lover.*

80 Draft: salutary. *The end of virginity is…*

81 Var.: a *second* life; a *new* life.

can save her. I do not believe we should, at[82] supreme times like these, worry about the proprieties and hesitate. But I will come back to see you tomorrow, I am in too much of a hurry today, and we'll talk again.'[83]

Françoise remained alone for a few minutes, thinking about the doctor's words, but soon involuntarily began thinking again about the mysterious correspondent who had been so cleverly bold, so brave[84] when it was a question of seeing her, and when he had to obey her, so humbly renunciative, so gentle. The idea of the extraordinary decision he must have made to attempt this adventure out of love for her filled her with joy. Already she had asked herself several times[85] who it could be, and now she imagined it was a soldier. She[86] had always loved them, and old passions, flames that had been denied nourishment because of her virtue, but that had set her dreams on fire and sometimes made strange reflections pass through her chaste eyes, were rekindled. Long ago she had often wanted to be loved by one of those soldiers whose broad belt takes long to unbuckle, dragoons[87] who let their swords

---

82 Var.: *in.*

83 Draft: we'll talk again. *But for [now] quickly.*

84 Var.: who had *braved so many dangers.*

85 Var.: *often.*

86 See, following the present text, a development begun here and forming a story different from the present one.

87 Var.: *artillerymen, chasseurs.*

drag behind them in the evening at street corners[88] while they look elsewhere and when you clasp them too close on a sofa you risk pricking your legs with their big spurs, soldiers who all hide beneath a too-rough cloth for you to easily feel a careless, adventurous, gentle heart beating.

Soon,[89] just as a wind moist with rain loosens, detaches, scatters, rots the most fragrant flowers, the sorrow of sensing the loss of her friend drowned all these voluptuous[90] thoughts beneath a wave of tears. The face of our souls changes as often as the face of the sky. Our poor lives[91] drift[92] at whim between the currents[93] of a voluptuousness where they dare not stay and the harbour of virtue that they don't have the strength to reach.

A telegram arrived. Christiane had taken a turn for the worse. Françoise left, and arrived the next day[94] in Cannes. At the villa rented by Christiane the doctor did not allow Françoise to see her. She was too weak for now. 'Madame,' the doctor finally said, 'I don't want to reveal[95] any of your friend's life to you; I know nothing about it in any case.

---

88 *behind them*: interlinear addition.
89 Var.: *But* soon.
90 Var.: *evil.*
91 Draft: lives *are both voluptuousness.*
92 Draft: drift *from voluptuousness to virtue.*
93 Var.: *enchanting stories.*
94 Var.: the *evening.*
95 Var.: *betray.*

But I think I should tell you one fact that might make you, who know her better than I, guess the painful secret that seems recently to be oppressing her, and in that way bring her some appeasement,[96] or, who knows, perhaps even a remedy.[97] She keeps asking for a small box, dismisses everyone, and has long conversations with the box, which always end in a kind of crisis of nerves. The box is there, and I have not dared open it. But given the invalid's extreme weakness, which might at any time become of great and immediate seriousness, I think it might be your duty to see what it contains. In that way we can know if it's morphine. There are no injection marks on her body, but she could be swallowing it. We cannot refuse to give her this box; her emotion when we resist is such that it would soon become dangerous, possibly even fatal. But we would be greatly interested to see what we are bringing her all these times.'

Françoise[98] thought for a few minutes. Christiane had confided no secret of the heart to her, and she would certainly have done so if she had had one. It must be morphine or some similar poison; the doctor's interest in finding out[99] was pressing, immediate. With little emotion she opened

---

96   Var.: *relief.*

97   Draft: perhaps. *It's a kind of letter she keeps asking for, staring at it, she sends everyone else away stays with.*

98   Draft: *Chris.*

99   *doctor's… finding out*: interlinear addition.

it,[100] saw nothing at first, unfolded a paper, remained astonished for a second, let out a cry and fell. The doctor rushed to her; she had only fainted. Near her lay the box that had fallen from her hands, and next to it the paper that had fallen out. On it the doctor read: 'Go away, I order you.' Françoise soon returned to herself, had a painful, violent contraction all of a sudden, then, in a voice that seemed[101] calm, said to the doctor: 'Imagine that I thought I'd see laudanum, in my emotion. I am mad.[102] Do you think,' Françoise asked, 'that Christiane can be saved?' 'Yes and no,' the doctor replied. 'If one could suspend this languid state, since she has no diseased organ, she could recover completely. But there is no way of telling what could stop it. It is unfortunate that we cannot know the sorrow – probably due to love – from which[103] she is suffering. If it were in the power of a person currently living to console and cure her, I think, [that person] would[104] perform that duty even at great cost.'

Françoise immediately had a telegraph form brought to her. She wired her confessor to come by the next train. Christiane spent the day and night in almost complete somnolence.[105] Françoise's arrival had been hidden from

---

100 Draft: opened it, *looked*.

101 *that seemed*: interlinear addition.

102 Draft: mad. *'There was nothing but this piece of paper,' said the doctor.*

103 Var.: *and* from which.

104 Draft: *could not*.

105 Var.: Christiane *was quite calm.*

her. The next morning she was so poorly, so agitated, that the doctor, after getting her[106] ready, had Françoise come in. Françoise approached, asked[107] her for news so as not to frighten her, sat down by her bed and gently consoled her with deliberately chosen, tender words. 'I am so weak,' said Christiane, 'bring your forehead close, I want to kiss you.' Françoise had instinctively recoiled, but fortunately Christiane didn't see this. Soon she overcame her emotions and kissed her tenderly and at length[108] on her cheeks. Christiane seemed better, more animated, wanted to eat. But a servant came to whisper a word[109] into Françoise's ear. Her confessor, the Abbé de Tresves,[110] had just arrived. She went out to talk with him in a neighbouring room, cleverly, without letting him guess anything. 'Abbé, if a man was dying of love for a woman, who belongs to another woman [*sic*] and whom he had the virtue of not trying to seduce, if the love of this woman could alone save him from a near and certain death, would it be excusable to offer it to him?' Françoise asked quickly. 'How could you not know the answer yourself?'[111] said[112] the Abbé. 'That

---

106 *after getting her ready*: interlinear addition.
107 Var.: *cheerfully* asked her.
108 *and at length*: interlinear addition.
109 Var.: came *to speak*.
110 *the Abbé de Tresves*: interlinear addition; other possible reading: *Treste*.
111 Var.: How *can you hesitate*.
112 Var.: *replied*.

would amount to taking advantage of an invalid's weakness, to sully, ruin, prevent, annihilate the sacrifice of his whole life, which he made for the sake of his conscience, and for the purity of the woman he loved. It is a fine death, and acting as you say would be to close the kingdom of God to someone who deserved it for having triumphed so nobly over his passion. That would be above all[113] for the woman too pitiful a fall to join the one who without her would have cherished his honour beyond death and beyond love.'

Françoise and the Abbé were summoned: Christiane, dying, was asking for confession and absolution. The next day Christiane was dead. Françoise received no more letters from the Stranger.

---

113 Draft: above all *to someone who would deprive God of such a joy.*

THE MYSTERIOUS CORRESPONDENT

[Unfinished Variation]

[Françoise's dreams about the soldier who might be the mysterious correspondent formed the basis of a separate story covering four handwritten pages, which we transcribe here. The heroine remains anonymous; unlike the one in the previous story, she is a widow burning with a stifled sensuality. To describe this, Proust develops a very lengthy military-themed metaphor – long before the Great War that would inspire the author of In Search *with the symbol of military strategy. The role of artistic culture, especially Botticelli, foreshadows the atmosphere of 'Swann in Love'; the (Wagnerian?) collaboration of all the arts holds painting, music and literature in equilibrium (eventually these will be represented by Elstir, Vinteuil and Bergotte). The heroine vanishes behind the complacent portrayal of a handsome soldier, one apparently she would like to conquer, another Phaedra facing a new Hippolytus ('she saw him, she loved him'). The presentation of this potential love of a young woman for an officer evokes the subject of* Anna Karenina, *and we know that the first period of Proust's creative life, including* Jean Santeuil, *has an affinity*

with the Russian novel. Incidentally, we will see, in this germ of a new story branching off from the initial story, a war with the Iriates, the name of a people in the region of Milan, around the city of Iria in Liguria, situated somewhere vaguely between Antiquity and the medieval duchy. A contemporary reader thinks, faced with this indeterminacy, of the stories of Julien Gracq.]

I ndeed before deciding on virtue,[1] at the age of uncer-
tainties, she had had a very keen taste for soldiers. She
loved artillerymen, whose belts it takes a long time – ah!
such a long time – to unbuckle, and the dragoons who
in the street at night[2] let their swords drag while looking
away, and who on a sofa when you clasp them too closely
risk pricking your legs with their big spurs – all of them,
really, lancers, cuirassiers, chasseurs who all hide beneath
a cloth that's too thick for you easily to feel a carefree,
adventurous, pure, gentle heart beating.[3] Then[4] the horror
that her parents would experience upon finding out about
it and despairing; the desire to keep the good position
in society that she occupied;[5] and more than anything

---

1   Var.: before *deciding on honesty*.
2   *at night*: interlinear addition.
3   *for... beating*: interlinear addition.
4   Draft: Then *the fear of*.
5   Var.: that she *should occupy*.

the uncertain nobility of her character[6] that would have prevented him [*sic*] both from renouncing an[7] adventure imposed by chance and attempting an adventure only[8] offered preserved her virginity intact. She had got married, but had been widowed after two years. Now the senses were taking their revenge[9] not directly,[10] but treacherously, by weakening her thinking, corrupting her imagination,[11] by casting over all her most disinterested ideas a seductive, deceptive velvetiness, by perfuming even the most austere things with an odour of love, kindling enough flames in her to make mirages of desire gleam in the desert of her heart – and[12] by[13] this slow degradation of her will[14] made her experience in her morality losses more costly than[15] if they had made her experience a seemingly more serious defeat on the battlefield of behaviour. The extreme artistic, literary and musical culture with the help of which she had refined[16] the most painful voluptuousness, a rare natural[17]

---

6 Var.: the nobility *of* character.
7 Var.: of *getting out of* an.
8 *only*: interlinear addition.
9 Draft: *revenge over her re[ason]*.
10 Var.: not *on the battlefield of behaviour*.
11 Between the lines: *by weakening her thinking*.
12 Draft: and *by overexciting*.
13 Var.: *in*.
14 Var.: *of her imagination*.
15 Draft: than *if she had taken a revenge*.
16 Draft: refined *the voluptuousnesses*.
17 *natural*: interlinear addition.

distinction of mind, during the ample leisure times a virtuous widowhood provides, had gathered together, harmonized, increased all her tendencies. These were all her strengths, all her energies, all her merit. Slowly all of that was in the process of passing over to the enemy. It was then that, after our little war with the Iriates, a twenty-three-year-old captain,[18] Honoré,[19] became in three years major, colonel, commander-in-chief.[20] He[21] had never agreed to have his photograph taken, but the newspapers and a few portraits by masters[22] had made his mysterious beauty popular without simultaneously rendering it commonplace. The languishing smile of his red[23] lips that nonchalantly bit each other the way one nibbles on a flower; the absolute perfection[24] of his features; the sadness; the light and dark areas; the gentle authority of his greenish[25] eyes; his hair, short on the sides but abundant beneath his kepi, glowing and bright as a child's hair; the slimness of his waist with

---

18 Var.: *lieutenant*.

19 Next to Honoré between the lines, one can read the name *Nowlains*; see below, the General of Notlains.

20 Drafts: in-chief. *His intelligence passed for He passed for a Napoleon of decadence, of as [subtle] delicate an intelligence as that of great captains long ago was vigorous. Photograph.*

21 Draft: He *had* agreed.

22 Between the lines: *all the public and military ceremonies*.

23 *red*: interlinear addition.

24 Var.: *purity*.

25 Draft: greenish, *his shining childlike hair*.

its pronounced hips; the inimitable grace,[26] abstract and meaningful as that of a Botticelli, of a [*gap*] as elegant[27] as that of Brummel and just as sensuously intoxicating as that of a courtesan – all of this mingled in him[28] to create such a voluptuous plastic perfection and such a captivating power that they seemed enemies he had conquered. Thought usually lines the eyes admirably, hollows out depths in the gaze, but wilts the complexion, bends the waist. General de Notlains had escaped these laws.[29] Before seeing him she wanted to love him; she saw him, she loved him, and by dint of thinking about him had given him her imagination and without making it too specific so as not to dissipate his prestigious mystery a perfect [*breaks off*].

---

26 Between the lines: *the elegance*.
27 Var.: as *knowledgeable*.
28 Var.: *gave him*.
29 Draft: *human* laws. *She saw him*.

A CAPTAIN'S REMINISCENCE

[Unlike the other stories we're publishing here, this story was previously published. Bernard de Fallois gave a faithful transcription of it in Le Figaro *on 22 November 1952 (p. 7). It was then reproduced by Philip Kolb, though he had been unable to consult the manuscript, in* Les Textes retrouvés de Marcel Proust *(Urbana, University of Illinois Press, 1968, pp. 84–6; reprinted Paris, Gallimard, 'Cahiers de Marcel Proust', new series, No. 3, 1971, pp. 253–5). Since certain parts of the text were heavily crossed-out and rewritten, one will note minuscule modifications here as compared with the previous version; these are explained in the list of variations.*

In this reminiscence, the affinity of two men is suggested but never named outright. Too close to Proust's personal experience, perhaps in connection with his military service in Orléans, from 15 November 1889 to 14 November 1890, this story was abandoned. The silent meeting between the captain and the corporal constitutes the most complete section of the story, unlike its long introduction, made of poorly linked additions that struggle to make a coherent whole.

67

As Bernard de Fallois notes, the allusion to 'Olympio's Sadness' (he wanted to see everything again) would eventually be brilliantly developed by the Baron de Charlus, in Sodom and Gomorrah: *'It's so beautiful, the time when Carlos Herrera asks the name of the château by which his barouche is passing: it is Rastignac, the home of the young man he once loved. And then the Abbé falls into a reverie that Swann, who was very witty, called the "Tristesse d'Olympio" of pederasty' (Recherche, Vol. III, p. 437). One can find this expression in Notebook 1 of 1908 (Carnets, p. 32); one can see that the idea without the phrase goes back much earlier here. The captain studies his attitudes towards the corporal like the Baron de Charlus observing the hero in Balbec (Recherche, Vol. II, pp. 110–12), and is fascinated by the young soldier, also like Charlus when he sees the violinist Morel in uniform at the Doncières train station (Recherche, Vol. III, p. 225). Finally, the captain's farewell on horseback to the corporal prepares the way in negative for the strange, indifferent salute that, in* The Guermantes Way, *Saint-Loup would give the hero from his tilbury, after a stay at Doncières where, paradoxically, he had been warmly received: 'and, leaving at top speed, without a smile, without a muscle of his physiognomy moving, he was content to keep his hand raised for two minutes to the edge of his kepi, as he would have replied to a soldier he didn't know' (Recherche, Vol. II, p. 436).*

But the originality of the story is to portray in the first person a feeling of homosexual emotion without even identifying it, at least consciously, as demonstrated by the whys? *that arise from his telling of the facts, as well as the sorrow that ensues. Later on, a sketch of* Sodom and Gomorrah *would make explicit the link between this unconscious emergence of homosexuality in the character and what would become the main subject of* In Search *(the story of a calling): 'When one is young one knows one is homosexual no more than one knows one is a poet' (*Recherche, *Vol. III, p. 954).*

Although the draft is less developed than its story, the captain's general reflections should keep our attention because they reveal a meditation on memory and the re-creation of reality by thought, which insistently tries to take form. There result interesting intuitions about future 'lost time', through 'which laziness and something like a little genie of the subconscious and of "non-thought" make us lose'. The philosophical speculation nourished by Proust's studies underlies these developments, contrasting, as in Fichte, what is inside *the self with what is* outside *the self. ('Outside ourselves? Inside ourselves would express it better,' the narrator of* In Search *would write – Vol. II, p. 4). We see here already the consequences for the development of this story, experimenting with two opposite narrative options, to compare the speculative effect Proust could draw from it: depending on which section is crossed out, the captain asserts either that he* sees again very well *or* no longer sees clearly *the figure of the corporal. The whole future of Proust's speculative novel lies inside these precious hesitations.]*

I had come back to spend a day in the little town of L.,
where I served as lieutenant for a year; I desperately
wanted to see everything again, the places that love[1] made
me incapable of thinking back on without a great shudder
of sadness, and the places,[2] although so humble, like the
walls of the barracks and our small garden, adorned only
with the various graces that light bears with it according
to the hour, the mood of the weather and the season.
Those places[3] remain forever, in the little world of my
imaginations,[4] clothed in great sweetness and beauty. Even
though I might have gone for months without thinking
about it, all of a sudden I see them, as at the bend in a
rising path one sees a village, a church, a little wood,[5] in

---

1   Draft: love *made unforgetta[ble] to me*.
2   Var.: the *other* places.
3   Var.: *Those forever.*
4   Var.: *daily* imaginations.
5   Var.: a *field.*

the lilting light of day. Barracks, courtyard, garden where in the summer my friends[6] and I would dine,[7] the memory surely painted with that delicious coolness the enchanting light of morning or evening would bring. Every little detail is illumined there and seems beautiful to me. I see you as from the hill. You are a little world that is enough unto itself, that exists outside myself, that has its sweet beauty, in its so-unexpected clear light. And my heart, my cheerful heart of that time, sad for me now and yet cheering up, since for a little while it[8] delights the other one, the sick and sterile heart of today,[9] my cheerful heart of that time is in that sun-filled little garden,[10] in the courtyard of the barracks[11] so far away and yet so close, so strangely close to me, so inside myself, and yet so outside myself, so impossible to reach ever again. It is there in the little town full of lilting light and I can hear[12] a clear sound of bells filling the sun-drenched streets.

So I had gone back[13] to spend a day in that little town of L.… And I had felt less keenly than I feared the sorrow

6   Var.: *comrades* (word crossed out).
7   Draft: would dine, *courtyard of the barracks*.
8   Draft: it *convinces an instant*.
9   Draft: of today *in its cheerfulness*.
10   Var.: *luminous*.
11   *of the barracks*: interlinear addition.
12   Var.: and *that is why* I can hear.
13   Var.: *returned*.

of finding it less[14] than I found it sometimes in my heart, where already I found it too rarely anywhere, which was truly sad, and at times, despairing... We have so many fertile opportunities to despair, which laziness and something like a little genie of unconsciousness and of 'non-thought' make us lose. — So I had found again the great melancholies among men in the things of that place. And also the great joys[15] that I could scarcely explain and that only two or three friends can share since they so completely lived my life in that time. But here is what I want to tell. Before going to dinner, planning to take the train straight afterwards, I had gone[16] to give an order to my old regimental orderly[17] to send some forgotten books. He had been assigned to the other regiment, barracked at the far end of town. I met him in the street at that almost deserted time[18];[19] in front of the little door of the barracks of his new regiment, and we chatted for ten minutes there in the street, all lit up by the evening, with[20] our sole witness the corporal on sentry duty who was reading a newspaper

---

14 Draft: less *in itself, than it.*
15 Var.: also *little joys.*
16 Draft: gone *to say.*
17 Draft: orderly *at the barracks.*
18 Draft: deserted time; *he had just left.*
19 Semicolon in the MS.; there should be a comma instead.
20 Draft: with *only seated on a sentry stone.*

seated on a cornerstone, against[21] the little door.[22] I can no longer see his face very clearly,[23] but he was very tall, a little thin with something deliciously refined and gentle in his eyes and mouth. He exercised over me an entirely mysterious[24] seduction and I tried to pay attention to my words and gestures, attempting to please him and to say things that were somehow admirable, either in their delicate meaning, or by much kindness or pride. I forgot to say that I was not in uniform,[25] and that I was in a phaeton[26] that I had stopped to chat with my orderly. But the corporal on guard must have recognized the phaeton of the Comte de C., one of my old comrades[27] in the same year we were promoted to the rank of lieutenant, who had placed it at my disposal for the day. My[28] old orderly, moreover,[29] ended each reply with *mon Capitaine*, so the corporal must have been perfectly aware of[30] my rank.[31] But it is not at all[32] the custom for a soldier to present arms

---

21 Var.: *in front of.*

22 Draft: *The face I don't see very clearly.*

23 Var.: *well.*

24 Draft: *inexplicable* seduction.

25 Var.: that I *did not have my* uniform.

26 Draft: and that I was *inside* a phaeton.

27 Var.: *one of my friends.*

28 Var.: *What's more* my.

29 Draft: moreover *replying very fre[quently] after each.*

30 Var.: *could not be unaware of*; draft: perfectly *that I was.*

31 Var.: perfectly *who I was*; my rank.

32 Draft: at all *to make.*

to officers wearing civilian clothes, unless they belong to[33] his regiment.

I sensed the corporal was listening to me, and he had lifted his exquisite[34] calm eyes towards us, which he lowered to his paper when I looked at him. Passionately desirous (why?) for him to look at me, I inserted my monocle and pretended to look everywhere other than in his direction. The time was growing late, I had to leave. I could no longer prolong the conversation with my orderly. I said goodbye to him with[35] a friendship tempered expressly with hauteur because of the corporal, and looking for a second at the corporal who, seated on his stone, kept his exquisite calm eyes raised towards us, I saluted [him] with my hat and head,[36] smiling a little at him. He stood up very straight and held his right hand open against the visor[37] of his kepi, without letting it fall, as one does after a second for the military salute. He continued to look at me fixedly, as is the rule, but with an extraordinary agitation. Then, while getting my horse going, I saluted him entirely as if he were already an old friend to whom I expressed in my gaze and my smile infinitely affectionate things. And

---

33 Draft: belong to *the same*.
34 *exquisite*: interlinear addition.
35 Draft: with *enough haughtiness*.
36 Draft: *I completely raised my hat*.
37 Var.: *glued to the* visor.

forgetting reality, by that mysterious enchantment of gazes that are like souls and that transport us into their mystical realm where all impossibilities are abolished, I remained bare-headed, already carried quite far away by the[38] horse,[39] my head turned towards him until I couldn't see him any more at all. He was still saluting and truly two gazes of friendship, as if outside of time and space, of friendship already trusting and well established, had met.

I dined sadly, and remained in real anguish for two days; in my dreams that face suddenly appeared, sending shivers through me. Naturally I never saw him again and I will never see him again. But in any case now you see I can no longer clearly recall his face, and it seems to me only very gentle in that warm square turned blond by the evening light, a little sad though, because of its mystery and incompleteness.

---

38 Var.: *my*.

39 *already… horse*: interlinear addition.

JACQUES LEFELDE

(THE STRANGER)

[Here is another story involving an enigma, which will never be resolved since the story lacks an ending. Why does Jacques Lefelde return every day to the same spot? Why does his sadness transform one fine day into joy? The manuscript breaks off before giving us the answer.

These reveries in the Bois de Boulogne around the lake seem to foreshadow the final sequence in Swann's Way: *'At the end of last August as I was crossing the Bois de Boulogne…' you will read here. But the Rousseau-like experience stretched out in the boat will not reveal its mystery. The writer's name, 'Jacques Lefelde', was chosen because no actual writer is recorded with this name.*

The enigmatic strolls of the young writer at the Bois evoke similar scenes described by Proust's friends, especially Reynaldo Hahn, telling about his long solitary lingering in front of a Bengal rose bush ('Promenade', in L'Hommage à Marcel Proust, La Nouvelle Revue Française, *No. 112, 1 January 1923, pp. 39–40).*

But this inconsolable lover, whom we always find at the same corner of the garden, evokes more precisely the story by Stendhal, in Chapter XXIX of On Love, *portraying a Comte Delfante who seems in fact to be an alter ego of Stendhal himself, described this way in Lombardy: 'In a laurel thicket in the Zampieri garden that overlooks the path I was following and that leads to the Reno waterfall in Casa-Lecchio, I saw the Comte Delfante; he was dreaming deeply, and although we had spent the evening together until 2 a.m., he barely returned my greeting. I went to the waterfall and crossed the Reno; finally, three hours later at least, passing again under the thicket at the Zampieri garden, I saw him again; he was in exactly the same position, leaning against a tall pine that rises above the laurel thicket.' (*On Love, *edited and introduced by Henri Martineau, Paris, Armand Colin, 1959, pp. 111–12.) Delfante was absorbed in the thought that his love was not shared. This is what Proust, in a letter to Daniel Halévy from 1907, calls 'those demonstrative little stories that Stendhal puts into* On Love' (Correspondance, Vol. XXI, p. 619).

Jacques Lefelde would later make an anonymous reappearance in In Search, *at Combray, in the stroll by the Guermantes way, along the Vivonne: 'How many times have I seen, have I wished to imitate when I'm free to live as I like, a rower, who, having put down his oar, had lain down with his head facing the stern, flat on his back on the bottom of his little boat, letting it drift with the current, able to see nothing but the sky flowing slowly above him, and wearing on his face the foretaste of happiness and peace.' (Recherche, Vol. I, p. 168.)]*

I would no longer meet[1] Jacques Lefelde, since I left for Passy leaving the Pont des Arts where he still lives[2] [*sic*]. At the end of last August[3] as I was crossing the Bois de Boulogne[4] to return home around nine in the evening I saw Jacques Lefelde, who[5] was headed towards the Grand Lac; he saw me and immediately looked away and sped forward. Soon I saw him. You who have read his 'essays',[6] you know[7] the profound mind, the unique imagination[8] of Jacques Lefelde. But if you are not familiar with the affectionate gentleness of his character you will not understand how I immediately put aside any idea that he might

---

1 Var.: *saw*.

2 Var.: since *I've lived in Passy; since I no longer lived in the Pont des Arts neighbourhood. It's been three years One evening returning home by.*

3 Var.: *July*.

4 Draft: Boulogne *one late afternoon*.

5 Draft: who *was walking quickly*.

6 Var.: his *profound, strange* 'essays'.

7 Draft: know *what a rare mind*.

8 Var.: *the strange* imagination.

be angry with me, and merely supposed he was going to some rendezvous. The following days were very fine; I continued going home on foot. Every day I encountered Jacques Lefelde, every day he avoided me. At the bend in Reine Marguerite lane, I would glimpse him again pacing slowly back and forth, as if he were waiting for someone; he would look everywhere, sometimes would lift his head to the sky like a lover. On the fourth day I lunched at Foyat[9] with a friend of Jacques, who told me that since his break with the little dancer Gygi, a break during which he had tried to kill himself, Jacques had renounced women forever. You will understand why I smiled. The days following I did not encounter him. One morning soon afterwards I read in *Le Gaulois*: 'Our young and famous writer M.[10] Jacques Lefelde leaves tomorrow for Brittany, where he will stay for several months.'[11] That day I met him near the Gare Saint-Lazare. Since I would not be seeing him again before October probably, I stopped him. 'I'm sorry,' he said, 'but I'm leaving tonight at nine o'clock and before I have to come back to dine I want to go to the Bois de Boulogne so I'm going to take the ring train quickly...' I was not surprised but I said, 'You would travel more quickly by fiacre.' 'Alas,' he said, 'I

---

9 *Conjectural*: interlinear addition.

10 *M.*: interlinear addition.

11 Var.: where *etc.*

have no more than twenty *sous* on me.'[12] I did not want
to be indiscreet but I said, 'I could drive you in my car,
and drop you wherever you like.' 'Well, I accept,' he said
with a cheerful, embarrassed air. 'But you can drop me
at the entrance to the lake, for I need to be alone.' At the
entrance to the lake he got out and I drove off in my car;
but I could not resist the desire to see from the parallel
lane the woman to whom my friend was coming to make
his farewell. Time passed, I did not see her arrive; Jacques
was strolling alongside the water, his head bent towards
it, sometimes lifting them [*sic*] towards a thicket and then
bringing them back to the water. Sometimes he walked
quickly, sometimes he slowed his pace; after half an hour
I saw him return, but not disappointed like a lover who
has waited in vain, rather with his head held high, his step
swift, his demeanour full of joy. I understood none of
it, dreamt about it, then stopped thinking about it. Last
year my friend L., who had been appointed [*conjectural*]
minister at XXX came to spend a month in Paris at the
hôtel on the corner of the Luxembourg Gardens. I would
go and visit [him] every day at his place, when one afternoon as I left him I met Jacques Lefelde, whom I hadn't
seen again and who seemed upset to meet me. He left me
quickly. I returned home unhappy. The next day at the

---

12 A phrase in the middle of the line: *there's no train before half an hour.*

same hour I found him again. He wanted to avoid me, I stopped him. The rain that had been threatening for a long time began to fall quite heavily, so we went into the Luxembourg Museum to take shelter.[13] 'I haven't seen you again,' I said to him, 'since the day when I had the pleasure of going with you to the Bois,' I said to him [*sic*]. 'May I ask you, without being indiscreet, what you were going to do there?' Jacques is very shy.[14] He blushed slightly. 'I'm going to seem stupid,' he said, smiling gently. 'But I'm going to tell you that when for the second time I dined at the chalet on the Île I was very sad. The lake of the Bois, which had never before impressed me, seemed to me so beautiful that the next day I couldn't resist the desire to go back to see it. For two weeks I was truly in love with it. I didn't know what path to take so as not to meet people of my acquaintance, for when I was not alone with it, it said nothing to me. And the day you drove me was the day of my departure. I did not want to leave without seeing it again. And also[15] I wanted before I left Paris to take stock of the year that had passed.[16] To give myself the strength to grasp it, understand it, judge it, nothing could equal

13 Draft: take shelter. *My friend I said to him I haven't seen you I said since the day when you kindly drove me to the Bois, I am very grateful to you, I owe [conjectural] you a great pleasure. Are you still going.*

14 *Jacques… shy*: interlinear addition.

15 Draft: And also *it was the last day of.*

16 Draft: passed. *Where could I better.*

the melancholy exaltation I tasted by the shore of that
beautiful water I was so enamoured of and where that
evening the sky was resting so sadly between the swans
and[17] the passing boats[18] as well as my mind detached from
the earth between the lawns[19] and the flowering borders,
even more intense at that moment that follows the sunset,
violently[20] real. Since the young boatman[21] was letting his
companion row and was stretched out on the bottom, my
mind gave itself at once[22] the pleasure of speed and of rest
and slid with agility over surfaces as mellow and glorious
as that enchanted water, already cooled by night[23] and even
more burnished by the light.[24] The air was so sweet that it
floated over the water. And isn't the mind a little like the
air? However immense[25] the space is that you open in front
of it, it fills it. And the mind that suffers from being stifled
by an interlocutor, an interest, or a wall that is too close,
stretches joyfully, royally, freely in infinite perspectives[26]

---

17 Draft: and *the mists asleep*.

18 Var.: *sliding by*.

19 Var.: *greeneries*.

20 Var.: *strangely*.

21 Var.: *sailor*.

22 *at once*: interlinear addition.

23 Var.: by *the evening*.

24 Draft: *light. By making me arrive in time in your car, you caused me a very
great Your mind has such Your mind is like the*.

25 Var.: *great*.

26 Draft: *spaces*.

and climbs effortlessly with intoxicating and melancholy speed back up the course of streams and years.'

'Can I bring you one more time,' I said to him, I [*breaks off*].

IN THE UNDERWORLD

[This discarded play is presented as a dialogue of the dead, or a dialogue of orators (between the biblical Samson, Jacques de Lévis de Caylus, and a contemporary of Proust's, Ernest Renan, who died in October 1892) about homosexuality. It is an academic exercise, representing and mimicking all the scholastic forms, on a subject forbidden to academic assignments compared to which Gisèle's final examination essay in Within a Budding Grove *(Recherche, Vol. II, pp. 264–8), in which Sophocles writes from Hades to Racine 'to console him for the failure of* Athalie*', will seem quite anodyne. Through the fluent oratory of the scholars, we also see the controversy between Charles and Brichot being prepared (here Caylus/Quélus and Renan), on the same subject, in* The Captive, *after hearing the septet at the Verdurins' (Recherche, Vol. III, pp. 800–13). The verses by Alfred de Vigny that will form the epigraph to* Sodom and Gomorrah *much later make their first striking appearance here. Poetry, described by this fictional Renan as 'divine madness', is akin to the felix culpa in which Catholic theology sees original sin, since it led to*

redemption. The title of the play, 'In the Underworld', superimposes the ancient concept that permits this dialogue of the dead about the punishment that threatens reprobates like Caylus.

Many stories, published or not, attempt to make possible the confession of homosexuality during a deathbed scene that frees one from guilt in light of the end of life; a further step is taken here, imagining a pagan representation of the beyond, where one can talk at a distance, remote as a bright star, since there is no longer any human experience to live through, and talk about situations that go to the limit of the intolerable during a lifetime.

The context of Proust's youth makes its appearance several times. The name Quélus brings to mind the Comte de Caylus, a favourite of Henri III: the character appears, also spelled Quélus according to a tradition that goes back to Pierre de l'Estoile, at the occasion of the duel of favourites with Bussy, in La Dame de Monsoreau by Alexandre Dumas père (see Les Grands Romans d'Alexandre Dumas: La Reine Margoe, La Dame de Monsoreau, Paris, Robert Laffont, coll. 'Bouquins', 1992, pp. 1235–6 and 1257). Proust was familiar with this novel in 1893 (Correspondance, Vol. I, p. 245; he deplores the play drawn from the novel) and he reread it in 1896 (Correspondance, Vol. II, p. 106). Even more so, the concept developed by Samson comes close to the theory that Proust expounded to his comrades as a lycée student (including Daniel Halévy) at the Lycée Condorcet, but who found him too insistent: 'I have very intelligent friends, of great moral delicacy, I flatter myself, who once amused themselves with a friend... it was the beginning of youth. Later on they went back to women. [...] I will readily tell you about two Masters of great wisdom who in life gathered only the flower, Socrates and Montaigne. They allow the very young to "amuse themselves" in order to experience all pleasures a little, and to let the overflow of their tenderness come out. They thought that these friendships, at once sensual and intellectual, were worth more than liaisons with stupid, corrupt women when one is young and when one has a keen sense of beauty and also of the "senses".' (Correspondance, Vol. I, p. 124.)

The family milieu also casts its shadow over these pages. Albuminuria, the medical example chosen by Quélus, was a recurrent disease on Proust's maternal side. And the doctors' considerations on the madness of poets were formulated not long before Adrien Proust published L'Hygiène du neurasthénique in 1897; in The Guermantes Way, Docteur du Boulbon's tirade on the link between disease and genius will correct this initial point of view (Recherche, Vol. II, pp. 600–01).

But these possibly mad poets offer the advantage (is it emphasized?) of changing our point of view *about things*. This is the first time (with no example by Giraudoux to help him yet) that there appears from Proust's pen what will be, in The Guermantes Way (Vol. II, pp. 622–3), the 'new writer' (le 'nouvel écrivain'). The modern woman, whom we will see mentioned here, will become the woman painted by Renoir found in the street, or the Parisian like Albertine, on whose shoulders

*Fortuny placed a cloak drawn from a painting by Carpaccio in Venice (*Recherche, *Vol. IV, pp. 225–6).*

In this way the budding writer endows this oratorical, humorous dialogue with a rich resource that has only to wait for novelistic contexts to be developed in many different ways.]

Quélus passes by. Samson stops two passing shades and points out Quélus. Would you do me the honour of introducing me? One of the two shades: Which one should we introduce? The other: To Quélus because of his title. Samson: No, introduce him to me, I am the elder. The first shade: Call Quélus. The Comte de Quélus. Monsieur Samson. Quélus: Sir, I have heard much about you during my earthly life. Samson: The order of time kept me from reciprocating. No doubt without that I would have spent my captivity amassing secret documents about you. You interest me infinitely, Monsieur. What's more, I had predicted it to you, what did I say: woman will have Gomorrah and man will have Sodom, And casting an irritated gaze from afar, the two sexes shall die, each in a place apart. Quélus makes a slight gesture of assent,[1] in the elegant bow of a society gentleman. Samson: Ah Monsieur, how

---

1   Var.: *bows slightly.*

93

right you were,[2] and if I and everyone else had acted as you did, no doubt Delilah would have shown herself to be more easy-going. But it is not as[3] coquetry, indirect homage made to feminine grace, that I approve these boys' games. It is something a man would do to have banished far from us this being less human than animal, strange substitute for a pussycat, bizarre cross between viper and rose, this woman perdition of all our thoughts, poison of all our friendships, of all our admirations, of all our devotions, of all our religions; thanks to you and men like you,[4] love is no longer a disease that places us in quarantine from all our friends, prevents us from talking philosophy with them. On the contrary it is only a richer[5] flourishing of friendship, the joyful crowning of our tender fidelities and its virile outpourings. It is, like the dialectic and the wrestling matches of the Greeks, an amusement to be encouraged and that strengthens, rather than loosens, the bonds that unite men to their brothers. But my heart finds an even more profound joy in finally contemplating you, Monsieur. What a confidant I have found for my resentments against womankind; we will be able to unite our resentments, curse them all together. The curse, such

---

2   Var.: *are*.

3   Var.: *by*.

4   *and men like you*: interlinear addition.

5   *richer*: interlinear addition.

a delicious action, perhaps unfortunately, since to curse someone is a little to evoke her, it is to live again a little with her. — I would like, Monsieur, to be of your opinion, but I cannot do so. Never has a woman disturbed me, and I understand neither the obscure attachment that in your rage binds you nevertheless to her by painful, trembling, tangible threads – nor the strong indignation she inspires in you. Incapable of discussing with you the spells[6] of woman, I feel even more incapable of detesting her with you. I have some bitterness against men, but I have always infinitely appreciated women. I have written pages about them that people have called sensitive and that were at least sincere and true. I have counted trustworthy friends among them. Their grace, their weakness, their beauty, their minds have often intoxicated me with a joy that, owing nothing to the senses, was no less intense, while it was purer and more lasting. I would go to them to console myself for the betrayals of my lovers and there is some sweetness in weeping at length and without desire against a[7] perfect breast. Women were both Madonnas and nurses to me. I adored them and they cradled me. The less I asked of them, the more they gave to me. I paid court to several of them, a homage imprinted with a wisdom that was undisturbed

---

6   Var.: *seductions*.

7   Var.: *alongside*.

by the squalls of desire. In exchange, they would give me exquisite tea, ornate conversation, a friendship that was disinterested and gracious. I can scarcely be angry with the ones who by a cruel, slightly silly game wanted, by offering themselves to me, to make me confess that I had no taste for them. But even without full-fledged pride, the most elementary coquetry, the fear of compromising their charm with such a sincere admirer, a little kindness and generosity of mind discouraged such an attitude in the best of them.[8]

Monsieur Renan passes by. Be quiet, hack. How can one believe in fact[9] that there is not in your discourse the proud artifice of the theoretician but rather[10] the approximate[11] summary of your [thinking]. At the very most you have hidden yourself from loving women, like those guests who scorn the finest fruit presented them. They ate before coming to the banquet. But you have unquestionably loved women. Believe me, my dear friend, that there is in these words no reprimand,[12] however philosophical on my part,

---

8   Var.: discouraged *it* among the best of them. Here there is a paragraph crossed out: *A philosopher passes by. Be quiet, Quélus, and do not speak of women with a detachment that you did not always have. What's more, you are about to appear before the Judge, and you would do better to repent. Indeed.*

9   *in fact*: interlinear addition.

10   *rather*: interlinear addition.

11   Var.: *exact faithful.*

12   Var.: *no criticism.*

and do not see in my reproaches the irrevocable condemna-
tion of an over-absolute morality. How, without deserving
to be taxed with narrowness of mind, could we clumsily
refuse to comprehend games about which Socrates spoke
with a smile. This Master, who loved Justice to the point
of dying for it, and so to speak at the same time bringing
it into the world, good-humouredly tolerated in his closest
friends these practices that today are outdated. And since
distance in space imitates distance in time rather well, it
will not seem absurd to say that even today the Orient, so
interesting from so many other points of view, remains[13]
the poorly extinguished hearth of these strange flames. In
any case, love, as the Ancients thought of it, is unquestionably a disease. How then can we compare these customs to
a vice? There's no doubt that albuminuria would take on
none of the marks of immorality if among certain people
its result was a production of salt rather than sugar in the
urine. Despite these reasons, the thought of absolving
you, my dear friend, is far from me. You have been clumsy
twice. Inexpiable crime if, as I am inclined to believe, life is
rather a game of skill. It is not very good, from any point of
view, to take one's pleasure by stroking one's time against
the nap. A man who being endowed [with] the most usual

---

13   Var.: *is.*

configuration of the palate would, however,[14] take on the habit of finding the most exquisite treat to devour[15] from excrement would be received with difficulty, at least in good society. Certain physical repulsions are stronger than anything and are given a mark of infamy. Inevitably our disgust and our esteem could not go to the same people. And yet who would dare say that disgust is not eminently relative?[16] Why turn away from the most exquisite perfumes offered you and instead lean over the mouth of a sewer, convincing yourself that you are breathing in a flowerbed. A posture assuredly neither[17] more nor less based in the absolute than the stance of the lover of gardens and perfumes – but a strange posture, which relies only on a physical disposition of the nerves of the nose, and which, you can be sure of it, will be very widely noticed. But you have committed a graver blunder[18] for it implies an error over a wider circle, over a more subtle degree of knowledge. Love, I have said, is a disease. But cerebral exaltation or madness is also a disease. There is no doubt, though, that the day poetry made its appearance on Earth it radically raised the level of madness. Almost all poets are madmen. Who,

---

14 *however*: interlinear addition.

15 Var.: to *take* the most exquisite *dish*.

16 Sentence crossed out: *The most exquisite fruits are within your reach, it is imprudent to pass them up.*

17 Var.: *Strange* posture, *although neither.*

18 Var.: *fault.*

though, would dare to speak ill of them? They are sick, say the doctors, characters who are obviously overrated but among whom I, however, count infinitely distinguished, cherished friends. What's more, by showing us dying, do they not contribute notably to enlarging the circle of our acquaintances and shifting (strong suffix[19]) the point of view of our meditations? And so doctors say quite reasonably about poets that they are sick, mad. So be it. But fortunate disease, divine madness as the mystics say. The appearance of woman, especially of modern woman, on Earth has in a like manner considerably expanded the utilitarian but quite limited career that love seemed destined to make on Earth in its early days. The opulent woman, synonymous with consolation and enthusiasm, has truly made of love a sublime disease that you could only lower by eliminating that prime factor, my dear Quélus. The difference of sex is all-important here. To whom can we attribute, apart from her, this refreshment that comes to us from our love for a being so different from us, a refreshment so similar to the peaceful days of a city worker spending his holiday in the countryside? Finally, this romanticism, by making her play an even greater role in edifying poetry, has definitively endorsed mental alienation in people of taste. In the same way, ever since the eighteenth century, it seems to me that

---

19 Conjectural reading.

your error has become a heresy, woman having become divinely perfected, and having enriched herself with all the delicacies that the most refined minds revere. Today she is an object of art and luxury that can no longer fear competition. It is true that you claim to taste[20] delicate pleasures with her and to satisfy your senses elsewhere. What a pointless, clumsy complication of existence. The pleasure of your senses would be enriched and refined by all that woman alone can give to our imagination. What's more, is this separation you speak of even possible? What force can prevent us from embracing the woman we admire so much? And I would like to add other words to the word 'embrace' that might shock the discourse of a philosopher, which is already sufficiently extensive.

---

20 Var.: *take*.

AFTER BEETHOVEN'S
EIGHTH SYMPHONY

[This text, written on two pages, plays on the puzzle story: we think we're reading a lover's monologue, until the very last words rearrange the meaning of the whole piece. Proust seems already to have been introduced to Schopenhauer's theory, which would so effectively nourish the musical descriptions of the compositions by Vinteuil. According to Schopenhauer, the listener to a piece, having in an exceptional way been brought face-to-face with the voice of the Will by music, applies to this voice the Representations that provide him with his fantasy, and thus instinctively places melody and image in relation with each other, without which nothing could justify this relationship. A philosophical substratum shows very discreetly through these lines: the elusive essence in its manifestations, form escaping its matter (Aristotle), the infinite reduced to the finite (Schelling). But the allusion to Christ's words, My kingdom is not of this world, *surrounds these considerations with a* fin-de-siècle *aura that can be found in epigraphs throughout the entire collection of* Pleasures and Days.

Psychoanalysis might interpret the word refouler, *repel or repress, in relation to Proust's asthma, as the images of the air that we breathe, filling space or encountering limits and walls, in a context of desire that is reciprocated or is not communicated. Another scriptural allusion, to the promise made by the angel to* men of good will, *will eventually reappear in* The Fugitive, *when the hero of* In Search, *having arrived in Venice, sees the Angel of the Campanile and thinks with melancholy of that promise, which for him is still unaccomplished (*Recherche, *Vol. IV, p. 202). In the meantime, the whirling melody of Vinteuil's sonata will have embodied for Swann this elusive essence of love, beyond life. Faced with this transitory beauty, the young listener of today meditates on the phenomenon of charm; much later, the Baron de Charlus wants to re-baptize the violinist Morel as Charmel.* Fantasy, which here rebuilds the kingdom of music, is the remote ancestor of the *age of* beliefs *that will eventually be the first stage in the evolution of the hero of* In Search.*]*

W e sometimes hear about the beauty of a woman,[1] the friendliness or uniqueness[2] of a man, the generosity of circumstance,[3] promising us[4] grace. But soon our mind senses that the being who made these delicious promises was never in a state to keep them, and it impatiently struggles against the wall that repels it; just as[5] the air that, like the mind, always aspires to fill ever vaster spaces[6] rushed in as soon as a wider field was opened to it,

---

1   The beginning has several drafts: *Sometimes in the brilliance of a woman's beauty, in the perspectives opened to us by the friendliness of a man or; Sometimes in the middle of the fires with which a beautiful woman radiates, in the future; We sometimes hear, in a low voice, from a woman among us, indistinct and present, so false that often we wonder afterwards if we heard it in dream. Sometimes the beauty of a woman, the friendliness or uniqueness of a man, the prestige of a circumstance, [murmur] to us very quietly, like these words, misunderstandings which we think.*

2   *or uniqueness*: interlinear addition.

3   MS: circumstances *murmur to us, in an indistinct voice* [crossed out].

4   Var.: *murmuring promises to* us.

5   Var.: *as thus.*

6   MS: spaces, *if after having.* Another draft: *If a space where air is contained grows larger, the air rushes in and occupies it completely.*

and was again compressed. One evening I was the dupe of your eyes, your walk, your voice.[7] But now I know exactly how far that goes, how close the limit is, and the time you stop saying anything, letting your eyes shine brighter into space, for an instant like a light that can't be maintained[8] for long at that degree of brightness. And I know too, dear poet, how far your kindness for me goes and whence it comes, and also the law of your originality, which, once discovered,[9] allows us to foresee steady surprises and to draw the seemingly infinite from it. All the grace you can give is there; it cannot increase with my desire, cannot vary according to[10] my fantasy, cannot unite with my being, or obey[11] my heart, or guide my mind. It is a boundary stone. I had scarcely reached it and I have already passed it. There is, however, a kingdom[12] of this world where God willed that grace would keep the promises it made us, came down so far as to play with our dream, and lifted it to direct it, lending it Its form and giving it Its joy, changing and not elusive, but rather growing and varied by possession itself, a kingdom where a gaze of our desire immediately gives

---

7   MS: voice. *They have.*
8   Var.: *leave.*
9   Var.: *known.*
10 Var.: *with; to* my fantasy.
11 Var.: *command.*
12 Var.: *world.*

us a smile of beauty,[13] which is changed[14] in our heart into tenderness and which it gives back to us infinitely, where one feels without movement the vertigo of swiftness without the weariness[15] or exhaustion of struggle, without danger the intoxication of sliding,[16] leaping, flying, where at any moment force is matched by will, desire with voluptuousness, where all things rush over every instant to serve our fantasy and fill it without wearying it, where as soon as a charm [is] felt, a thousand charms are joined to it, all different but conspiring, grasping in our soul [*sic*], in a mesh that is tighter, vaster and sweeter by the minute: that is the kingdom of music.

[Two separate handwritten pages could be attached to this parable. Schopenhauer's doctrine about music is here adapted to a compensation for the incommunicability between souls.]

Sometimes a woman or a man lets us glimpse, like a dark window that is vaguely illumined, grace, courage, devotion, hope, sadness. But human life is too complex, too serious, too full of itself and somehow too weighty,[17] the human

---

13 Var.: *gaze that we give with a smile and that is sent back to us.*

14 MS: beauty, *then a gesture.*

15 Var.: *danger.*

16 MS: sliding, *swimming.*

17 *too serious… weighty*: interlinear addition.

body with its many expressions and the universal history
it bears written on it, makes us think of too many things
for a woman ever to be for us. Unmitigated grace, unbri-
dled courage, unstinted devotion, limitless hope, unmixed
sadness.[18] In order to taste[19] the contemplation of these
invisible realities that are the dream of our life, and so that
we do not have just the shiver of their presentiment when
faced with women and men, we would need[20] pure souls,
invisible spirits, genies who have the swiftness of flight
without the materiality of wings giving us the spectacle
of their sighs, their fervour or their grace, without incar-
nating it in a[21] body.[22] For if our body too could enjoy this,
the play of its spirits would have to be incarnated,[23] but
in a subtle body, without size and without colour, at once
very far from and very close to us, which gives us,[24] in the
deepest part of ourselves,[25] the sensation of its freshness
without there being any temperature, of its colour without it being visible, of its presence without it occupying

---

18 Draft: unmixed sadness. *In order for us to feel more than the shiver of their*
    presentiment, we would need (see below).

19 Var.: *to have*.

20 Draft: *it would be necessary for us to have*.

21 Var.: *their*.

22 Drafts: body. *In order for our body to be able to enjoy this feast, in order for*
    the feast to be more intoxicating.

23 Between the lines: *the feast would be more beautiful*.

24 *us*: interlinear addition.

25 *-selves*: interlinear addition.

any space. Withdrawn from all the conditions of life, it would have to be swift and precise as a second of time; nothing should retard its momentum, prevent its grace, weigh down its sigh, stifle its moan. We know in this exact, delicious, subtle body the play of these pure essences. It is the soul clothed in sound, or rather the migration of the soul through sounds; it is music.

THE AWARENESS
OF LOVING HER

*[This is a heavily edited text, written on two pages. This story is the mirror image of Edgar Allan Poe's poem 'The Raven' with which Proust was familiar (*Correspondance, *Vol. X, p. 91), in which a young man suffering from solitude sees a raven enter his room; it keeps answering 'Nevermore' to his complaints, and pushes him to the point of despair. Here the lover's suffering is externalized as a silky animal whose companionship (invisible to others) consoles the rejected lover.*

The narrator, however, remains objective enough to suggest that for him a whole lifetime of similar solitude has passed: and so the comfort is mitigated and possibly poignant. In this way, this brief text is linked to the 'end-of-life' stories present in this collection. The same is true for this character in a society novel (later on, in 1909, Proust would read Ginette Chatenay *by Georges de Lauris, a model of the genre), awakened by his servant, stepping into a fiacre – like Swann, later on.*

An intense ambiguity imbues these lines, between the beloved's expressed or implied rejection, the allegorical identity of the squirrel-cat ('you' is replaced with 'it'), the consolation or the companionship in despair brought to the solitary man by his secret companion. Proust hesitates between third-person analysis and direct speech; the two replace each other or overlap in the rewritten sentences, with direct speech allowing an entrance in medias res *into the psychological problem, which the dialogue-writer of* In Search *will remember later.*

The servant who awakens the main character in his solitude here foretells the valet de chambre *awakening Swann after his dream, at the end of 'Swann in Love', and also Françoise announcing to the hero that 'Mademoiselle Albertine has left', at the turning-point of both* The Captive *and* The Fugitive.

The author of Pleasures and Days *projects a lover's torment that cannot be articulated here in the fable of a mysterious animal, one emanating from a musical world as well. From the title, 'The Awareness of Loving Her', onwards, this text prepares the way for the moments of awareness in the development of the hero of* In Search, *and his circulation in society as being inhabited by an inner preoccupation that escapes everyone else.]*

N ever[1] never I repeated those words to myself that she had said to me and that, by[2] the terrifying silence of the waiting[3] that had preceded them and the despair that had followed them, had made me for the first time hear my heart that was uttering with equal stubbornness these words always always. And now, one wounding the other to death, these two refrains alternated desperately and I kept hearing them so close, so profoundly like those throbs that relentlessly beat the depths [*sic*] of deep wounds. So when my servant entered to tell me the car[4] was waiting and that it was time to go[5] and dine [he] shrank back in

---

1   Another beginning that was crossed out in the MS: *I had just realized for the first time with perfect clarity that I loved her and that, probably, I was not loved and might never be loved and that it was very likely I was never loved. And so.*

2   Var.: *in.*

3   MS: the waiting *that had followed* [crossed out].

4   Var.: *that a fiacre.*

5   Var.: was waiting *in order* to go.

alarm when he saw the front of my dress shirt dampened[6] with tears.[7] I dismissed him, got changed and prepared to leave.[8] But soon I realized that I was not alone in my room. A kind of cat-squirrel, half-hidden by the curtains around my bed, appeared to be waiting for me. It was clothed in white fur, with a hint of crested grebe. It had narrow blue eyes, and the tall white plume of a bird atop its head. 'God!'[9] I cried out. 'Will you let me die in this deserted world since her absence constantly makes the most complete void in it, in this desperate solitude. Won't you forgive me as you forgave man in the first days of the Earth. Let her love me or let me stop loving her. But one is impossible and I don't want the other. Make some light shine as in the first days on my tears.' The clock chimed eight o'clock. Afraid of being late,[10] I quickly left my room and climbed into the fiacre. In one supple, silent leap, the white animal came and snuggled between my legs with the calm fidelity of someone who would never leave me again. I looked for a long time[11] at its eyes where the deep, clear blue of endless skies seemed captive, spangled with

---

6   Var.: *soaked*.

7   Phrase crossed out between the lines: *He had had the negligence to leave the door open*.

8   Var.: and *left*.

9   This passage was added between the lines, up to *Afraid*.

10 Var.: *I rushed down the stairs*.

11 Var.: *more closely*.

a golden cross. Seeing them caused in me an irresistible,
infinitely bittersweet desire to cry. I went in without wor-
rying about you any more, beautiful white squirrel-cat,
but having arrived at my friends' house[12] scarcely had I sat
down at table, feeling so far from her and among people[13]
who did not know her, that an atrocious anguish seized
me. But immediately I felt against my knee a powerful,
gentle caress. With a swift movement of its[14] furry white
tail, the animal settled itself[15] comfortably at my feet under
the table, and like a stool[16] it held up its silky back.[17] At a
certain point I lost my shoe and my foot rested on its fur.[18]
From time to time, lowering my eyes,[19] I quickly met its
bright, calm gaze.[20] I was no longer sad, I was no longer
alone, and my happiness was all the more profound since it
was secret.[21] 'How is it that you do not have,' said a lady to
me after dinner, 'how do you not have some sort of animal

---

12 *having arrived at my friends' house*: interlinear addition.

13 Var.: among *so many strangers*.

14 Var.: *your*.

15 Var.: *you settled yourself*.

16 Var.: *cushion*.

17 Var.: back *to support both my feet*.

18 Var.: fur, *I felt consoled*.

19 Var.: *my head*.

20 Var.: gaze, *and I was proud and consoled by this precious treasure unknown to all who had come to me. 'You have a pretty animal there' my friend said to me.*

21 Var.: *unknown. Kindly animal without a sound how you have kept me company [in my life] during my life that you have mysteriously and melancholically adorned.*

to keep you company, you are so alone.' I threw a furtive glance under the armchair where the white[22] squirrel-cat was keeping itself hidden and I stammered: 'True, true.' I fell silent, I felt tears rising to my eyes.[23] That[24] evening as I was dreaming, running my fingers through its fur peopled my solitude with so many gracious, sad companions that I could have played some melodies by Fauré right there and then.[25] The next day I gave myself over [to] all my ordinary occupations, I walked down indifferent streets, I beheld my friends and my enemies with a rare, sad voluptuousness. The indifference and boredom that tinged all things around me had dissipated ever since there perched on it [*sic*] with the elegance of a bird-king and the sadness of a prophet the white squirrel-cat that followed me everywhere. Dear, kindly, noiseless animal, how you have kept me company during this life that you have adorned with such mystery and melancholy.

---

22 MS: *blue*.

23 Var.: rising *to the edge of* my eyes.

24 MS: Phrase added between the lines, up to *Fauré*.

25 Var.: *Franck*; *Schumann* [crossed out].

THE GIFT OF THE FAIRIES

[This half-backwards fairytale is about what good fairies say over the cradle of someone whose destiny is to suffer from an excess of sensitivity. We hear something like the interior monologue of the young Marcel Proust, hypersensitive and held captive by disease: the fairy externalizes his resigned pact faced with such a life. The gift, the subject's inner genie, is reminiscent of the daimon, *the inner being who lives inside Socrates in Plato's* Apology, *on which we can find notes by Proust in his school papers.*

Part of this situation will remain in the very last sequence in Time Regained, *the 'Masked Ball' (*Bal de têtes*) section, with the narrator of* In Search *insisting on the enchanted aspect of this final society reception that resembles a masked ball. Note here the way in which self-analysis gradually replaces the fairytale. This dialectic of the magical and the realistic permeates the entire collection of* Pleasures and Days.

At issue are two disparate texts, whose state of development is different. The first prepares the way for the essay on Chardin and Rembrandt, but has not yet taken the form of a moral fable:

'Take a young man of modest fortune', etc. (Essais et articles, p. 372). We see a description of the gifts distributed by the good fairies. The character now becomes the theatre of illuminations that prepare for the illuminations, scattered throughout lost time, of the hero of In Search, up to the final revelations that a draft of Time Regained will call illuminations à la Parsifal (Recherche, Vol. IV, p. 1389).

On the other hand, fairies pour onto the future man of genius a whole life of suffering in perspective, enough to make the over-whelmed young man repeat Baudelaire's phrase: 'I have more memories than if I were a thousand years old.'

An acquaintance of Proust's, René Peter, wrote (his acquaint-anceship with Proust occurred quite a bit later, in 1906) that 'Marcel very much liked the expression "vieux" ('old man') in speaking of himself, as he aged in an exaggerated and almost laughable way' (Une saison avec Marcel Proust, souvenirs, Paris, Gallimard, 2005, p. 31). Proust, a thirty-five-year-old man stricken with 'this fictional age difference' (p. 32), wanted to establish that expression in dealing with others. Here we will read the origin of this habit, and its emotional reasons.

Renouncing the pleasures of going out is here contrasted with the contemplation of a tree, or a branch: Reynaldo Hahn gave a famous testimonial of this about Proust ('Promenade', in L'Hommage à Marcel Proust, La Nouvelle Revue Française, No. 112, 1 January 1923, pp. 39–40), which, after it has been transposed into fiction, makes the hero's exclamation all the more *poignant in* Time Regained*: 'Trees, you have nothing more to say to me' (*Recherche, *Vol. IV, p. 433), if they had to be the forced interlocutors of one who could not live fully.*

Above all, we will see sketched out with a strange clarity the situation of the hero of In Search *anxiously hoping to be able to find Gilberte on the Champs-Élysées. Here originally the narrator is described as finding a little boy, which explains her slightly rude manners, some of which will remain later on in Gilberte. One can examine the textual variations to discover how the fairy addresses a little girl, for this shift to allow her to hope keenly to join her friend.*

The second extract, in the tone of the texts discarded from the collection, is one of the documents that most intensely gives the biographical etymology of later fictional episodes.]

I t's when we are in our cradle that the fairies bring the presents that will make the sweetness of our life.[1] Some gifts we know how to use quite quickly and for ourselves:[2] it seems that no one needs to teach us how to suffer.[3] The same is not true for others.[4] Often a charming gift lies[5] deep within us, one we do not even know. And it's necessary for a good genie[6] to illumine the part of the soul where it is hidden, show it to us, teach us its powers. Often, after this sudden illumination, we let the precious present fall back into useless oblivion until another good genie comes back to raise it up and place it in our hands. These good genies are the ones generally called men of

---

1   Var.: will make *the joy or unhappiness* of our life *in so many others* [breaks off]. Draft: *We learn quite quickly how to use those who.*

2   *and… ourselves*: interlinear addition.

3   Draft: *But often others keep presents for a long time for us.*

4   Draft: *Most of us remain for a long time Deep within most of us.*

5   Var.: *is hidden.*

6   Draft: genie *comes.*

genius. To all of us who are not men of genius, how sombre, how gloomy life would be if there were never any painters, musicians or poets who lead us to discover the outer and inner world. This is the service given to us by these good genies, they reveal to us unknown forces[7] in our soul, which[8] we increase by using them. Among[9] these benefactors[10] I will praise today the painters[11] who make the world and life more beautiful for us. I know a lady who walked with her eyes closed after leaving the Louvre, so as not to see the ugliness of the passers-by and the streets of Paris after the perfect faces of Raphael and the woods of Corot. Genies could give her nothing beyond the fairies' gift, and indeed the gift of the fairies was of little peace to her. Speaking for myself, when I leave the Louvre I do not[12] leave the wonders, since I continue on or rather I am merely beginning, after this initiation: sun and shadow on rock, a glistening dampness on horses' flanks, a strip of grey or blue sky between houses, the very flush of life in the gleaming or rusty pupils of the people passing by. Today at the Louvre I paused especially before three painters who are not at

---

7   Var.: *unused treasures.*

8   Draft: which *grow.*

9   Var.: *Amidst.*

10   Draft: benefactors, *painters have.*

11   Draft: painters. *Who of us, having returned from visiting.*

12   Draft: I do not *emerge.*

all alike; each of the three has rendered me a wonderful, different service. They are Chardin, Van Dyck and Rembrandt.

A[13] fairy leaned over his cradle and said sadly to him:

My child,

My sisters have given[14] you beauty, courage,[15] gentleness. You[16] will suffer, though, since to their gifts I must, alas!,[17] join my own. I[18] am the fairy of misunderstood sensitivities. Everyone will harm you, wound you, the ones you won't love, the ones you will love even more.[19] Lighter reproaches, a little indifference[20] or irony[21] will often make you suffer; you will think of these as inhuman weapons, too cruel for you to dare use them, even against mean people. For despite yourself you will attribute to them your soul and your ability to suffer. In that way you will be defenceless. Fleeing the rudeness of men, you will

---

13 Beginning of the sentence crossed out on the top of the page: *Forced by inexorable fate.*

14 Var.: *brought.*

15 Var.: *virtue.*

16 Var.: *Despite these gifts.*

17 *alas!*: interlinear addition.

18 Var.: *And* I.

19 Drafts in the MS: even more. *You will be defenceless against mean people. Naturally lending them Perceiving their soul reflected in your own.*

20 Var.: *the most natural* indifference.

21 Var.: *the least bitter* irony.

seek out first the society of women, who hide so much sweetness in their hair, in their smiles, in their shapes and the perfume of their bodies. But the most ingeniously friendly of them will cause you sorrow without realizing it, wounds in the midst of caresses[22] and, while plucking painful strings, will scratch without knowing it.[23] They will not understand your tenderness any better when, by an excess of sensitivities and intensity, it gives rise to mad laughter or defiance.[24] Since others will not have in themselves the pattern for this suffering, or for this tenderness[25] that they will inspire in you without understanding them, you will be constantly misunderstood. Never will anyone be able to console or love you. But although it has been used up before having served its purpose, your body will not resist the repercussions of the impulses and matters of your heart. You will often be feverish. You[26] will not sleep,[27]

---

22 Var.: caresses, *just as cats bite in the midst of being stroked and scratch while they draw in their claws.*

23 Var.: knowing. *The slightest sympathy will do you good, will bring back your so-divided tenderness will be so much more subtle.*

24 Passage crossed out in the MS: *Keep it, however, [despite] without hoping [to meet] ever to make [heart] exchange with anyone. If they are not tender towards you, [someday you might give joy to an unhappy person by being tender to him] you will however have an opportunity to be tender, and you will generously spread this unknown, exquisite perfume at the weary feet of those who are suffering.*

25 Var.: tenderness *that you feel.*

26 Draft: You *will always be.*

27 Var.: You *will sleep poorly.*

you will be constantly shivering. Your[28] pleasures will thus be corrupted at their source. Even feeling them will hurt you. At the age when little boys[29] go out to laugh and play, you will always weep on rainy days because they will not take you to the Champs-Élysées where you will play with a little girl[30] whom you will love and who will hit you, and on sunny days when you see one another, you will be sad to find her less beautiful[31] than in the morning hours when, alone[32] in your room, you were waiting for the moment[33] to see her.[34] At the age when little boys[35] run feverishly after women,[36] you will be thinking all the time, and you will already have lived much more than very old people. So when, conversing with your parents,[37] you hear them say to you: Someday you will stop thinking about yourself, when you have lived more, when you have our experience, you[38] will smile modestly only out of deference. Those are the sad gifts I bring you, gifts I had no choice but to bring

---

28 Var.: *All* your.
29 Var.: *little girls*.
30 Var.: *a little boy*.
31 Var.: to find *him* less *handsome*.
32 Var.: *when she is alone*.
33 *the moment*: interlinear addition.
34 Var.: *him*.
35 Var.: *little girls*.
36 Var.: *become flirtatious*.
37 *conversing with your parents*: interlinear addition.
38 Draft: you *will shake*.

you, and which you cannot, alas, cast far away from you, breaking them; they will be the sombre emblems of your life until your death.

Then a voice made itself heard that was both weak and strong, light as a breath and like the limbo from which it came, but dominating all the voices of earth and air[39] by the gentle certainty of its accent: I am the voice of the one who is not yet but who will be born from your misunderstood sorrows, from your unrecognized tenderness, from the suffering of your body. And not being able to free you from your fate, I will penetrate it with my divine odour. Listen to me, console yourself, for I say to you: the sadness of your scorned love, of your open wounds, I will show you their beauty, so sweet that you will not be able to avert your gaze – damp with tears, but enchanted. The harshness, the stupidity, the indifference of men and women will turn for you into a diversion, for it is profound and varied. And it will be as if in the middle of the human forest I had lifted the blindfold from your eyes and as if you[40] paused with a joyful curiosity[41] in front of[42] each trunk, in front of[43] each branch. Indeed, illness

---

39 *and air*: interlinear addition.

40 Draft: you *paused*.

41 Var.: with *joy*.

42 Var.: *at*.

43 Var.: *at*.

will deprive you of many pleasures. You will not be able to go hunting, or to the theatre, or to dine in town, but it will allow you to attend to other occupations that men usually neglect, and that at the time you leave life you might deem[44] the only essential occupations. What's more, especially if I make it fertile, illness has[45] powers that health does not know. Those sick people that I favour often see many things that escape the able-bodied. And while good health does have its beauty which healthy people scarcely notice, illness has its grace, which will bring you profound joy. *[A sentence crossed out.]* Then resignation will be able to blossom in your heart that tears have soaked like the fields covered instantly in violets after April rains. Do not hope you will ever be able to exchange your tenderness with anyone. It is a substance that is too rare. But learn to revere it all the more. It is bitter and yet sweet to give without being able to expect anything in return. And if others are not tender towards you, you will often have[46] an opportunity to be tender to others, and you will generously spread, with the pride of a charity impossible to anyone else, this unknown, exquisite perfume at the weary feet of those who suffer.

---

44 Var.: *judge.*

45 Var.: *shows.*

46 Var.: *yet.*

[We can see now that Proust remembered this text when he wrote about Ruskin, in the article 'John Ruskin (second article)' that he gave to the Gazette des Beaux-Arts *on 1 August 1900: 'He was one of those "genies" whom even those of us who received at birth the gifts of the fairies need in order to be initiated into the knowledge and love of a new part of Beauty'* (Pastiches et Mélanges, p. 129).]

'THAT IS HOW HE LOVED...'

[This parable on the relationship between suffering and happiness returns to God the creator as a way of condensing the moral question by stripping it of its applications in society. When the hero of In the Shadow of Young Girls in Flower *enters the studio of the painter Elstir, the narrator emphasizes 'that if God the Father had created things by naming them, it was by taking away their names, or by giving them other ones, that Elstir created them anew'* (Recherche, Vol. II, p. 191). *The parable of migrating birds foretells the comparison the writer will make later on, between the development of an artistic vocation and the orientation of a homing pigeon.]*

T hat is how he loved and suffered all over the Earth, and God[1] changed his heart so often that it was difficult for him to remember[2] by whom he had suffered and where he had loved. Waiting for those moments[3] had been the obsessive preoccupation of his years, moments that always seemed only to be approaching[4] and that he'd have liked to possess beyond death – he could not find a trace of them the next year[5] in his memory, just as children do not find any traces of their castles defended with so much passion, after the next tide. Time like the sea carries everything away, abolishes everything, as well as our passions, not in its waves but under the calm, imperceptible, certain rise of its swell like children's amusements. And when he

---

1   Draft: God *had*.
2   Var.: *he could not remember*.
3   Draft: moments *awaited in fever*.
4   Var.: *never resolved*.
5   *the next year*: interlinear addition.

suffered too much from jealousy, God detached him from the woman by whom he would have liked to suffer all his life, if he could not be happy by her. But God did not want him to be like Him,[6] because He had placed in him the gift of song and did not want pain to annihilate it. So He set desirable creatures before him and advised infidelity. For He does not allow albatrosses, swallows, or other little songbirds to die of suffering and cold on the Earth they inhabit. But when the cold comes to seize them He places in their hearts the desire to migrate so that they do not fail their law, which is not to be faithful to the soil, but to sing.

---

6   Draft: Him, *and it was He who advised him.*